SEVEN OAKS

BY

FRANCIS JOHN BALDUCCI

THE LIBRARY OF CONGRESS
Control Number: 1-943964551

Balducci, Francis John, 1964–
seven oaks / Francis John Balducci

ISBN 061582885X
ISBN-13 978-0-615-82885-5

Front and rear cover designs, images and elements by the author.

Printed in the United States of America.

Dedication

To my wife, Daphne, and to our son, Robert.

Prologue

Under a billowing summer sky among the hovering oaks where the hidden multitudes of cicada chatter, a solitary Queen Anne Revival stands peacefully abandoned in its forested cul-de-sac. Nature seems to have thrived around the sizable structure; ivy creeps up on all its sides. The newly-posted and unsullied "For Sale" sign, however, protrudes in severe contrast to the surroundings.

A throng of wildlife inhabits the grounds—squirrel, raccoon, chipmunk, opossum, whitetail deer, and the occasional black bear—free from human abatement. Crevices that compromise the house's interior serve as an entryway for many of these creatures.

A dirt and gravel driveway leads away from the house and drains into a main road where a bright, thriving community awaits in stark contrast.

The small New England town, all too typically, boasts the standard business establishments: a hardware store, a pub, a coffee shop, and a pharmacy among others. Next to the town hall and police station stands a library and, across the street, a church. Although modern amenities can be found therein, in some ways—due to its old-fashioned character and charm—the town itself stands contrary to the twenty-first century world that it inhabits.

* * *

The house at Seven Oaks features faithful architecture with three-storied asymmetrical construction. Originally built in 1914, it has maintained some of its former charm despite the weathering and neglect. Its color schemes, once rich, are now chipped, worn and dull. As a result, the front façade offers a sorrowful example of its bygone self while resembling a facial expression that is tattered, somber and tired.

Typical of the architectural style, the house displays steeply-pitched roofs with complex, irregular plane shapes and overhangs, prudently-patterned vertical clapboards with fish-scale shingling in the gables, and long, narrow oriel windows. In the corner of the front façade, a turret rises topped with a cone-shaped dome and a decorative finial. The chimney boasts ornamentally-patterned masonry. A wrap-around covered veranda from the front and around the side is supported by narrow Doric columns with decorative spindle work. Carefully-designed steps and a balustrade-spindled banister, although in need of new color, prove welcoming under a prominent

Palladian window and a forward-facing gable that features the frieze of a grinning cherub.

While inside, the exposed rafter-beam construction above that includes a prominent central ridge beam remarkably resembles a human ribcage.

Chapter One

Mr. Lewis sports a gangling appearance while standing at the top of the steps in the warm September sun. An unlit cigarette occupies the corner of his wrinkled mouth. He seems older than he actually is. Fourteen years as a real estate agent and, during that time, all he had to show for his labor is two failed marriages, a young son of whom he never sees, a bleeding ulcer, and an on-again, off-again battle with nicotine. It has been three years since he showed the Queen Anne and, while a luxury sedan pulls into the driveway, he remembers much of his original pitch. He plans on moving south and retiring after selling a few more houses. Completing the next sale would accelerate these plans.

The Donegals have been married for four years. As the husband emerges from the automobile—a man of thirty years—he displays a casual appearance with attire affordable to a newly-successful venture capitalist. The quality of her clothes—a woman slightly younger—is similar in formal, social status but with splashes of color. Mr. Lewis smiles broadly toward them while he extends his hand.

"Bob—call me Bob."

"Jacob Donegal. Katherine, my wife," he said while gesturing to her.

"It's nice to meet you both. Well, here it is! I know it looks rather menacing, but, I assure you, it has great potential for charm. Let's step inside."

While they enter into an open foyer, Jacob and Katherine detect a foul odor.

"This house has been vacant for three years, correct?" Jacob said with a grimace from the stench.

"Yes," Mr. Lewis said. "The economy hasn't been helpful, so the bank lowered the sale price. You're happy with the price, right? I mean, it's a steal."

They continue on to a fully-furnished, sizable main parlor; large covers, dusty with age, are carefully spread over the furniture. Jacob carefully lifts one cover slightly to look, but he remains expressionless. They proceed toward the rear of the house. All around them, the rather irregular floor planning from room to room disrupts their expectations.

"The home has good flow," Mr. Lewis said.

"Really," Katherine said sarcastically.

Eyeing above, Jacob notices the central beam. He remains fixed on it as he walks. Ahead, the party faces the rear of the house. After passing under a small arch, they find themselves in the kitchen.

"No bells and whistles," Mr. Lewis admitted; "but, you can always modernize." The illuminated doorway off the kitchen leads to the neglected rear yard. Staring out into the yard, the Donegals offer a collective gasp.

"Again, potential," Mr. Lewis said with confidence. "C'mon, let's step outside."

While in the rear yard, they notice an isolated garden enclosed by a waist-high, wrought-iron fence with spear-like points over its arched gate. The gate appears rusted and encrusted with dried droppings.

"I don't think the previous owners gardened much," Mr. Lewis said while considering the unfavorable growth. "But, I'm sure you'll give it a try. You might find it relaxing." Katherine conveys a disinterested look.

Two hundred feet from the rear of the house stands an out-of-place structure. Rather than asserting an ornate appearance as the house, this edifice is purely utilitarian. Mr. Lewis notices Jacob staring at it.

"That's the garage," Mr. Lewis said. "It was built a few years back, where a barn once stood."

The garage door windows are so darkened by time that even a flashlight could not illuminate the interior. A loud screech pierces the warm air as the door is raised up high. Before them, the center of the space is occupied by a large, canvassed-covered object—a car. Mr. Lewis was never aware of this occupant. Jacob reaches and lifts the cover off revealing a 1957 Chevrolet convertible sedan in its original larkspur blue. It appears to be in fair condition.

"Is this included?" Jacob asked with elevated enthusiasm.

"A Bel Air?" Mr. Lewis said. "This car's a classic. I guess the assessor missed it. Well, let's just keep this between us and consider it a house-warming gift," he assured. "The bank doesn't need to know."

After a quick inspection of the car, Jacob considers the possibility of restoring it. It would be among the many things he considers restoring or rebuilding as the party completed the tour of the property. It did not take long for Jacob and Katherine to agree to the purchase.

* * *

After the controlled chaos of signing a seemingly endless array of legal documents, the Donegals become the new owners of the house. The occasion is met with great enthusiasm from Jacob. Katherine, however, remains only somewhat interested.

As a result of the furnishings included in the home, many of their original belongings were given away. Among the items retained included the family bible given to them by Katherine's parents, Lloyd and Constance Whittendam, as a wedding present. Jacob, not a follower of any organized religion, tolerated inclusion of the book as well as Katherine's unstable Nebelung cat, Mitsy. Katherine would be equally tolerable of the inclusion of Jacob's German shepherd dog, Ranger. This will be the first time that these animals will share a living space, and both Jacob and Katherine had their concerns.

Chapter Two

The house experiences new life with the addition of the Donegals. Cardboard boxes were carefully arranged in the main parlor resembling a city in miniature. The aroma of freshly-brewed morning coffee and the sound of a television news broadcast radiates from the kitchen. Jacob sits at the table, sipping and reading, while Katherine retrieves a blackened remnant from a house-warming gift.

"Fucking toaster!" she exclaimed.

Jacob reads on intently—his eyes fixed on the pages of the business section. Ranger lies loyally at his feet.

"I asked you a question," Katherine said sternly.

"I'm sorry. What is it?"

"Toast? Oh, never mind."

Jacob stops reading and turns his attention to the television.

"IndustryOne Capital, a Wall Street-based asset management company that has recently been specializing in corporate leveraged buyouts..."

"Your company is on TV again," she said.

"...is receiving scrutiny by several citizen groups over their acquisition of Excelsior Manufacturing Company...."

"It's not entirely my company," he corrected her.

"IndustryOne claims Excelsior is a failing company vulnerable to industry competition, and liquidation may be the only feasible solution. Opponents to liquidation, however, claim that Excelsior supports part of a growing American industry, that it retains a somewhat strong market position with an established consumer base, and that IndustryOne had no intention of ever addressing the company's modest debt even while the company's estimated intrinsic value may be sizable enough to serve as adequate loan collateral. For more on this story..."

Jacob's attention returns to his reading. He gulps down his coffee from a chipped mug. He then gives an egg remnant to Ranger and lets the dog lick his fingers.

"Try not to come home too late. I need you to help me unpack," Katherine said while leaving the room.

As she trots upstairs, Jacob turns off the television and moves toward the front door. In the center of the parlor, Mitsy sits blankly staring at Jacob. Jacob hesitates, and then extends his middle finger toward the animal. Mitsy is unfazed by the gesture.

With a quick look in a small wall mirror, Jacob makes his exit. While opening the car door, Jacob stops. He is forced to look up at the frieze of the grinning cherub. He becomes transfixed. "Is the expression changing?" he thinks. The face seems to expand and dominate his perspective. It contorts and transforms into a grotesque lump before becoming a bloody splotch. After Jacob squints and rubs his eyes, he sees only the grin.

* * *

Eight years quickly passed since Jacob and Katherine first met as business students. Even though Katherine had a boyfriend at the time, and despite Jacob's middle-income background, little prevented the twenty-two year-old honor student from pursuing her. There was only one thing he was drawn to more than wealth, and that was Katherine. One night, Jacob's persistence paid off. While she attended a fraternity party without her man, Jacob made his move offering his charm and wit wholesale.

Katherine was born into great wealth and prosperity. Her father, Lloyd Whittendam—a man currently in his late sixties and the founding chairman of the highly successful Whittendam Investments— had always been critical of the men that Katherine dated—all but one, and Jacob was most certainly not the one. Some regard Katherine as aloof, but Jacob would never realize any of her imperfections. Equally, Katherine tolerated Jacob's atheism while she always held a strong belief in God and has always been a regular churchgoer. Yet, there is something more to Katherine's love for Jacob. Not only did he endeavor to make her feel special and free, but at the time she met him, she was becoming highly rebellious of her father. Lloyd is openly disapproving of Katherine's choice, and the more he rejected Jacob, the more that she was drawn to the new boy. Her love for him deepened until and shortly after their wedding. Then, Jacob became more and more absorbed with obtaining the American dream.

As what he thought to be an "appropriate" wedding gift, Lloyd bluntly refused to hire Jacob undeterred that the young man—a full academic scholarship winner—graduated with honors, or that he is now a member of the family. On his own, Jacob was hired by IndustryOne Capital where he quickly ascended the corporate ladder. Even with steadfast ambition and tangible accomplishments, Lloyd refuses to embrace Jacob by regarding him as someone from "the wrong side the tracks." Jacob reciprocates by regarding the old man as a "cantankerous fuck." Jacob believes that he is on his way to achieving the sort of financial wealth that would one day surpass those amounts achieved by Lloyd Whittendam. It is beyond mutual disrespect; it is war.

* * *

Deep within the gut of a glass and steel moloch known as the IndustryOne Capital Building, Jacob drives to his parking space. He hurries to the elevator.

"Good morning, Mr. Donegal," the garage attendant said.

Jacob pushes the button to "46," the top floor, nods at the attendant and offers him a two-fingered salute as the elevator door closes.

The upscale offices of IndustryOne Capital look almost antiseptic, with silvery-white interior columns and frameless glass walls. Walking hastily passed the receptionist, Jacob proceeds down a wide hallway.

"Good morning, Mr. Donegal," the receptionist said, but he had already passed her desk.

Meandering past a gathering of suited men, Jacob arrives at his office. The strong, mahogany door bearing the sign, "JACOB DONEGAL – TREASURER," makes a deep thud when it closes. He is securely insulated until the next executive board meeting, which starts in less than an hour.

Since his hiring by IndustryOne Capital seven years prior, Jacob had steadily rose in ranks to become a key player. He considered all of his professional accomplishments with pride, but since the general economy had taken a downturn, he had concerns about the direction the corporation was taking. While ponding this and while staring at some reports, a knock comes to his door.

"Open!" Jacob called out.

"Jake! I heard we were on the news again. Bro, what the fuck?" Randall said.

Randall Neis, a few years younger than Jacob, serves as the controller. He is described by some as energetic, by others as deranged, and particularly by the women of the offices, disingenuous at best. He was hired two years ago and, despite his motley reputation, Jacob befriended him almost immediately.

"We're going after Excelsior? Are they that much in the shitter?" Randall cracked.

Ordinarily, Jacob would be annoyed with Randall's crude candor. However, Jacob was thinking exactly the same thing throughout his entire morning commute.

"I'm still reading up on this," Jacob sharply retorted as he gestures to some papers on his desk. "Come in and close the door." Randall does so and sits in one of the guests' chairs. He then scratches his arm vigorously as a rodent would.

"This is going to mean a lot of local jobs," Randall said; "but, fuck 'em! If you can't compete globally, you don't deserve to survive."

"Remind me why we're still friends," Jacob said without looking up.

"I'm serious. It's pure Darwinism, man." Randall changes direction. "Hey, I fucked a hot-looking Asian chick in the ass this weekend. She begged me to stop. She kept saying, 'Too big, too big!' Crazy bitch."

"Randall, please?" Jacob shot back. "Look, let's meet up for lunch later. I have to go through this stuff," he said as he lifts up the papers. "Okay?"

"Let's eat Thai," Randall said as he leaves the office. "I did."

Jacob feebly attempts to hide his smile from Randall, points to the door, and redirects his attention to the upcoming meeting. "Is there no rescue for Excelsior?" he ponders. He can't help but notice the irony of the company's name. "Over three thousand local jobs lost."

After twenty minutes of staring at numbers, Jacob heads toward the conference room. His curiosity heightens: "Based on the estimated intrinsic value of Excelsior Manufacturing Company," he thinks, "it may be sizable enough to serve as adequate loan collateral to keep it afloat." However, the board may look for the quick dollar. He tries to talk himself into not saying too much out of concern that, for the first time, he may not appear to be a team player.

In the ample, black-leathered, gray-carpeted conference room, the board members await the chairman and chief executive officer, Steven M. Storch. A man in his sixties, he survived the old-school capitalists to eventually evolve into a modern-day titan finding profits any way possible. He had shown Jacob much affection and allowed him increased access throughout the years, and he had once jokingly regarded him as "the son-in-law I never had." The door opens, and Mr. Storch appears carrying a black folder.

"Gentlemen, good morning," he said as he takes his seat at the head of the black lacquer table. "You all have the agenda. So, let's get started." The members open their folders as the door closes shut.

"Excelsior Manufacturing Company," he continued. "This company, with all intents and purposes, is either failing or is pretty damn close enough to it. Their white belly is exposed, and a leveraged buyout may allow us an opportunity to seize control and reap a profit. I say we finance the takeover with their low-quality debt and then sell off the equity. After we liquidate all of their assets, we then declare bankruptcy. It's that simple."

"So, there is no intention on addressing the company debt," Jacob said. "The debt is modest, and Excelsior is a growing industry."

"Maybe so," Mr. Storch said. "But, it's not growing dramatically enough. It's somewhat retaining a consumer base, but its market position is slipping. Manufacturers in China are closing in fast—too fast for them to keep up. The equipment Excelsior uses is steadily becoming obsolete. If we act quickly, we could also capitalize on unloading its intrinsic value before it diminishes to nothing."

"But, sir," Jacob urges. "This is a local company. What about all those factory workers?"

"Well, what about them?" Mr. Storch snapped.

After a brief silence, some members share grins at one another.

"Yes, Mr. Storch," Jacob said in an abdicating tone.

* * *

"It's gonna be hard getting used to all this traffic," Jacob thinks as he proceeds through a slight drizzle. His mind wanders. He thinks back on his life. In general, he considers whether he had made the correct professional decisions. Specifically, he thinks he said too much at the morning meeting. He also wonders if Randall is going mad.

Just as there appeared to be an opening in the curving road, red brake lights illuminate through the water beads on his windshield. Around a sharp turn and some green foliage, he sees the multi-color lights of police cruisers and an ambulance parked headlong on the shoulder. A grunt escapes his lips as he encounters the accident scene. But, as he draws closer, the seriousness of the event becomes increasingly clear to him.

"It's fucking mangled!" he said as he sees the wreckage. He looks closer to see that the entire front of the car is thoroughly destroyed. The windshield is gone. On the hood, a thick trail of blood streaked by the rain is plainly visible over the white paint color.

"C'mon! Let's go!" a squinting trooper said while redirecting Jacob's attention to an opening in the road. Behind the trooper, unseen to Jacob, a paramedic is carefully carrying an object in orange, plastic material. The paramedic slips, propelling the object onto the road in front of Jacob's car just as it accelerates. Before impact, Jacob sees a woman's decapitated head bounce in front of him. The head's long hair made it look like a large, playful ball of yarn. As he skids, he hears the knocking of the object reverberate on his car's undercarriage—under his feet—from front to rear. He dare not look into the rearview mirror. Rather, he accelerates again and heads for home. He cries out.

As he enters his driveway, Jacob's hands shake as he grips the steering wheel. They shook since the incident. He wipes the cold sweat from his forehead. His only saving grace after all, he considers, is that he did not kill someone. Just then, a tap comes to the side window. Jacob lets in a deep gasp.

"Oh, I'm sorry I startled you; I'm Jim your postman. I just wanted to say hello," he said.

Jim is a young man new to his job, and he received his postal route a few months before the Donegals arrived.

"Good luck with this house; I can finally see it now up close," Jim said with a smile.

"Just put the mail by the door, thank you," Jacob said while attempting to gain his composure.

After stepping out of his car, and as he closes the door, he looks up at the cherub. This time, it appears to smile at him.

Chapter Three

Under a cloudy November sky, the Donegals receive a special visitor. Jacob answers the door and immediately begins to shake: a police officer stands just outside.

"Mr. Donegal?"

"Yes?"

"Hello, my name is Harold P. Johnston; I'm the town's police chief. How are you doing today?"

Johnston appears to be a man in his forties, a veteran law-enforcement professional, wearing a well-pressed uniform with a shiny badge and numerous citations prominently displayed on his chest. Jacob tries hard to compose himself.

"What can I do for you, officer?"

"Well, I don't mean to intrude, but I just wanted to stop by and welcome you to our community. It's a fine house, and I certainly hope you find peace here."

"Oh, thank you," Jacob said with some relief.

"You're welcome," Johnston answered. "If you ever need me, I'm at your service. Have a nice day." Johnston turns and walks down the steps.

"You, too," Jacob said; he immediately closes the door and takes a deep breathe.

* * *

Unpacked and settled in, the Donegals begin to hang various pictures and items to fully make the surroundings their own. Katherine seems to be feeling at home; Jacob, on the other hand, begins to feel different than he did when they initially moved in. His enthusiasm has been replaced with puzzlement. The occupants experiencing the most difficulty, however, are the pets: Mitsy and Ranger.

Ranger is regarded by those who know him as a kind, stable animal with high intelligence. He is friendly to those who offer a friendly hand to pet him. Mitsy, on the contrary, is not well-balanced— according to those attempting to show manners. To those who are blatant, the cat is vile. Jacob notices that the cat has become increasingly violent towards both him and Ranger. While Jacob walks him, he notices some scratches on the dog's nose. Some are fresh with trickles of blood.

"What happened, boy?" Jacob asked him rhetorically as he examines the dog's injuries. "That evil, fucking cat!"

While Katherine sits on a chase lounge in the den reading a book, Jacob confronts her.

"Katie, your cat attacked Ranger."

"How? He can kill Mitsy," she returned.

"He's not that kind of dog," he retorted; "he has scratches on his nose. Some are deep."

Katherine puts the book on a small table and stands. She seems fatigued and off-balance as she holds her stomach.

"What's wrong?" he asked with genuine concern.

"I don't know. I've been feeling this way for a few days. I think I may be coming down with something. I'll be all right."

Before Jacob could ask her more, she goes into the bathroom and closes the door. Jacob then hears voices. As he turns, he realizes that they may be coming from inside his head. He steps outside to see if anyone is there. No one. He then looks up at the cherub. With his eyes slightly out of focus, the image appears to be contorted and grotesque. He rubs his eyes and then looks closer: the image appears to be grinning.

"Fuck you!" he called out to it, extending his middle finger.

* * *

Thanksgiving, and it is the day of Lloyd and Constance Whittendam's first visit to the house. The smell of roast turkey fills the place. Katherine planned a fine dinner while Jacob braces himself for sarcasm from his father-in-law and ignorance from his mother-in-law. He did much of the cooking, and he anticipates that his efforts will not be appreciated. But, he did it for Katherine.

"Nothing is ever good enough for their daughter—these fucking people," he thought as he gets ready.

At three in the afternoon, the doorbell rings. Katherine opens the door.

"Katie, dear!" Constance said with her arms outstretched.

"Hi, mom. Come on in." She takes a bottle of wine from Lloyd. "Thanks, dad." She kisses them both as they enter. "Let me take your coats. Jacob will be down soon."

"Oh, he still lives here?" Lloyd said sarcastically.

"Dad, please?" Katherine whispered to him. "Both of you have a seat in the parlor." They do so.

Jacob's anxiety increases with each step that he takes down the stairs. He clears his throat as he reaches the bottom.

"Hello Whittendams," Jacob said politely. "No need to get up," he said knowing all too well that they were staying seated. "Lloyd, how are you?"

"Yeah, fine," Lloyd said as he nods at him. He then directs his attention to Katherine. "Kate, you may want to open that bottle so it can breathe."

"Sure, dad," she returned. "Why don't we all sit at the table? Dinner's ready, and I'm sure you must be starving."

At the table, Jacob hopes that the time moves quickly while Lloyd stares down at the table and Constance wears a plastic grin.

"Excuse me," said Jacob; "I'll go help Katherine." He goes into the kitchen. After a few moments, they both return to the table with plates of food. They arrange the plates and utensils and take their seats.

"Let's dig in," Jacob said hastily.

"Wait, you don't say grace in this house?" Lloyd shot. "Let's bow our heads." They bow, and Lloyd says a prayer. All but Jacob and Lloyd close their eyes during grace.

"...Amen," Lloyd finished. "Okay, let's 'dig in' as Jacob so eloquently put it." Lloyd plunges a large serving fork into a mound of sliced meat. "You know, Jacob, you should pray more. Oh, that's right: you're—what do you call it?—an atheist?"

"Agnostic, actually," Jacob corrected him.

As their plates are filled and the serving plates are exchanged, Jacob attempts to change the topic by starting a conversation about IndustryOne and his successes there.

"Jacob, I've been meaning to ask you: I've read some things about Excelsior. Liquidation? I don't mean to quibble, but isn't that a bit extreme?" Lloyd said half-jokingly.

"Dad," Katherine interrupted.

"I'm being serious," Lloyd said while lifting a forkful of turkey to his mouth. Now, tell me: is this the sort of capitalism that your company now engages in? We don't build American companies anymore, huh?" he asked while he gestured with a knife. "We cut their heart out and let them bleed."

"Please don't point that knife at me," Jacob insisted.

"Albeit," Lloyd continues, "I suppose reinvesting in America is not the new agenda—compassion for your fellow man unimportant to the agnostic."

"Excuse me," Jacob stands; "I'm not hungry. I think I'll go for a walk."

"Jacob, don't!" Katherine demanded. But, before she could speak another word, he's gone.

* * *

In the kitchen, after dinner, Katherine and Constance converse.

"Mom," Katherine stops cleaning, "I think Jacob has been having a difficult time coping with our new surroundings; he's been tense all the time."

"Katie, dear, it happens," Constance said naïvely. "Let me have some more wine, quickly; your father doesn't want me drinking so much."

"What makes matters worse..." She hesitates.

"What dear?" Constance said after she quickly sips.

"I think I may be pregnant."

"Oh, Katie, that's great!" Constance puts down her glass and embraces her; Katherine continues to wear a worried look. "I'm going to be a grandmother!"

"Yeah, mom."

"Things have a way of working out," Constance reassured. "You have your health—your life."

"What do you mean?" Katherine asked.

"Did you hear what happened to Colton's wife?"

"No. What?"

"She was killed. She died in a horrible car crash a month ago."

* * *

While Jacob is out walking in the driveway, a rotted smell reaches his nose. He looks around for a few moments before being drawn to his car. Sniffing around, he looks underneath—at the rear axle. There, he sees a dark object wedged in between the housing. Using a crowbar from the trunk, he carefully pries the object free. Dropping to the ground and rolling toward him, he realizes that it is the human head that he encountered a month prior. He almost completely forgot about the incident. Holding his mouth in horror, he looks at the face. Although it is blackened and partially decomposed, he does make out some of the features. From what he can see, she looks familiar. She appears to have blonde hair. Grabbing a rag from the trunk, he picks up the object and thinks about what to do with it. Just then, he hears Katherine saying her good-byes to her parents at the front doorway. He panics. He runs to the rear of the house to evade them. He sees the garden gate. In his trepidation, he quickly determines that he cannot be found with this head; he does not want to be regarded as her murderer. He enters the garden, grabs the nearby shovel, and quickly digs a small hole. The head makes a deep, dull thud when he drops it in; just as hastily, he covers it with dirt.

"Who was she?" he thinks as he sat there—biding time until the Whittendams drive off.

Chapter Four

It is a week before Christmas. In the parlor, a broad, illuminated tree stands prominently. The smell of pine and beeswax candles permeates the air. There seems to be some holiday spirit in the home. In stark contrast, Mitsy is perched on the mantel; her eyes offer a green, evil glow.

In the kitchen, Katherine sips coffee, thinking of the future. She ponders whether Jacob is emotionally ready to have children. She peers out of the window, into the rear yard, and wonders why he wants her to keep out of the garden.

"He's become so distant," she thinks.

She looks over the mail of the table and finds an invitation to a holiday reception to be held at a neighbors' home. She wants to attend and hopes that Jacob will also be interested. She sees it as an opportunity for them to make new friends—local friends. Out of her recent loneliness, she no longer wishes to remain aloof.

* * *

In his office, Jacob looks over some profit projections. The company is growing. As a direct result, Jacob sees a dramatic salary increase.

While he looks over the Excelsior file, he notes that factory layoffs are pending and that the company will come to a complete shutdown in just a few weeks. A knock comes at his door.

"Jake?" said Randall; "you busy?" He enters.

Randall, dissolute as ever, sits and begins to tell Jacob about his lascivious weekend. Jacob grins but keeps reading.

"You're disgusting," Jacob said while still wearing a grin.

"Excelsior will soon be dead, huh?" Randall shifts while seeing the file that Jacob is reading. "That means a new boat for me. I mean, this is mad money for us, bro," he said while scratching his arm.

"Yeah," Jacob said without much enthusiasm. "Randall, how do you stay so alert and energetic?"

"Why?" Randall asked.

"Well, I can't seem to concentrate, and I'm fatigued all the time. Maybe I should exercise more."

"I think I have just the thing," Randall said; "but, you have to meet me later at my car."

* * *

At noon deep inside the building garage, while Jacob and Randall are inside Randall's sports car, and after they ingested some drive-thru burgers, Randall opens a small zippered leather case. A syringe and other medical items are neatly secured therein.

"Have you ever heard of methamphetamine?" Randall asked. "You know, meth."

"I've heard of it," Jacob answered with peaked interest; "but, I've never tried it."

Randall carefully removes the syringe, prepares a dose, ties his arm and exposes a vein. He then inserts the needle, draws in blood, and then injects the substance. He exhales.

"Now your turn," Randall said while regaining his composure.

"I don't know."

"C'mon, it's safe," Randall insists; "I'll set it up for you."

Randall carefully puts away his case, opens his glove box and removes a similar case. He prepares a dose while Jacob looks intently.

"Roll up your sleeve and tie this cord around your arm," Randall instructed. "I want to see a vein." Jacob complies. "You're going to feel a sting, but don't move."

Randall injects Jacob. After a few moments, Jacob starts to shiver. The effect increases until his body stiffens.

"Just relax," Randall said; "I didn't give you a full injection, so you should only be experiencing a partial rush."

"Oh, my!" Jacob said.

"What?"

"I—I like this," Jacob said while a smile slowly creeps to his face.

* * *

Katherine is not known for her homemaking abilities. Tonight, she attempts a pot roast; what she achieves is driftwood. Jacob slipped in the door a little later than usual, and took a seat at the mahogany dining table.

"I'm not terribly hungry tonight," he said as he looked at the hunk of brown, dried flesh.

"In that case, I want to talk with you," Katherine said with a somewhat desperate tone.

"Uh-oh, I've been a naughty boy again?" Jacob said sarcastically.

"My parents are very important to me," she said almost ignoring the sarcasm; "and you take them too seriously. They mean well."

"Can't they mean well without factoring me in all of this? Look, your father hates me! He thinks I'm a corporate whore and a Satan worshipper. I need to avoid this man! All I'm trying to do is carve out a life for the two of us—to make money and to do it the right way—to make our house a home."

Jacob gets louder.

"I'm not involved with what's going on with Excelsior" he said; "it's beyond my control! This fucking house!—There's something wrong with this fucking house!"

"Jacob, you're not making sense!" she pleaded.

"...and this holiday party coming up." Jacob picks up the invitation.

"What about it?"

"Since when are you so adventurous?"

"It might be fun. You remember how to have fun?" Katherine breaks down.

"Are you kidding? I'm always fun. I need fun! I'm not stuffy like other men—like Colton."

"Leave him out of this!" she demanded. "He's never done anything to you." Katherine starts to cry. "All that I want is to start a family with you; I want to be pregnant with our baby."

Katherine stops herself from saying any more. Jacob, realizing that he may have gone too far, embraces her. He looks down to see Ranger standing at his feet looking up at him. The dog whimpers.

"Let me walk him," Jacob said.

* * *

After a few days, in the evening, the holiday neighborhood reception is at its apex as Jacob and Katherine arrive. Bill and Mary Clarke, a couple in their sixties, greet them at the door and welcome them into their modest home. Katherine smiles and looks around at some of the other guests; Jacob makes an effort to be sociable by extending his hand to Bill. They shake hands.

"Let me take your coats," Mary said. "Drinks?"

"Red wine, thank you," Katherine said. "No, make that a ginger ale instead."

"Any beer, in the bottle is fine," Jacob said.

"You got it; there are some hors d'oeuvres going around," Mary said with a smile.

"So, Jacob, I'm glad you can make it," Bill said. "Let me introduce you both to the other guests."

Bill leads them into the parlor and gestures to the guests, introducing them, finally arriving at...

"...Lorenzo and his lovely girlfriend, Shelby," Bill concluded. "Just like you, they both recently moved to the area."

Lorenzo Carcione, a rather rotund man in his late thirties, is a self-made owner of a home-improvement company. Shelby, an attractive girl in her early twenties, quiet, stands in dramatic contrast to him way down to the cellular level. But, oddly, they are a couple.

Jacob anticipates that Lorenzo—an independent entrepreneur—is highly intelligent and worldly.

"Hey, dude! Great to meet you!" Lorenzo said while giving Jacob a bear hug—a greeting that does not make Jacob feel entirely comfortable. "Try the bacon-wrapped scallops; they're friggin' awesome!"

Jacob expects Lorenzo and Shelby to be a happy couple. Lorenzo has wealth. Perhaps, with a wedding on the way and a few children, Shelby could be set for life. However, the girl seems sad. Maybe she is shy and uncomfortable around people. She locks eyes with Jacob for a moment. She offers him a delicate smile.

"You bought the Cole house?" Bill said carefully to Jacob.

"Excuse me?" Jacob asked Bill.

"The Coles," Bill answers; "they lived in that house a few years ago."

"Oh, no. We never met them. They were nice people?"

"Ah, we didn't really know them too well," Bill said with some discomfort while Mary looked away. "Say, Jacob, can I show you something?" Bill shifts.

"Sure."

Bill leads Jacob to a private area in his house.

"I'm not sure if you're aware of this," Bill starts; "but, I work at Excelsior. I've worked for them for twenty-six years and I'm near retirement. My pension is in jeopardy. Now, I know you are a big-wig at IndustryOne. So, what can you tell me?"

"Look, Bill. I don't call the shots there," Jacob pleaded. "All I can say is what already has been publicized—that Excelsior is being targeted. Do you have savings? Investments? Your home is yours; it has equity."

"I paid into my pension throughout the years, and it will all be gone," Bill said with despair. "I was only allowed to invest in Excelsior. We were counting on all this money to carry us for the rest of our lives."

"Bill, I'm sorry..." Jacob said.

"There is no other work, and I'm going to lose my house; this kills me, Jacob!"

Jacob becomes very uncomfortable.

"Let's go back to the party, please?" Jacob insisted.

Jacob leaves Bill and goes back into the parlor to join Katherine. When he arrives, he whispers to Katherine that it is time to leave.

"It was nice meeting everyone, really," Jacob said to the other guests while putting his arm around Katherine.

"Thanks for coming," Mary said. "Let me get your coats."

While the Donegals move toward the door, Jacob looks back at Shelby. Her eyes never leave him as he walks to the door. She smiles at him. He smiles back. Katherine, unaware of the exchange, is putting on her coat. Before turning to leave, Jacob notices Bill standing at a distance. His face has the look of deep gloom.

* * *

Later this evening, just as they prepare for bed, Katherine conveys to Jacob that she is pregnant.

"You're pregnant. Oh, my!" Jacob said with noticeable fright.

"We talked about having children years ago. Well, it's going to happen. What's the problem?"

"It's just so unexpected. And, now, how am I going to fall asleep with this news?"

"You're acting ridiculous!" Katherine answered while holding back tears.

* * *

Jacob usually struggles with sleep. This night is no different. In a foggy dream, he hears a crying baby. He labors to see it, but he is unable to discern its features. The sound intensifies until it awakens him. While he sits, he still hears it, but faintly. The sound takes him downstairs where it gradually intensifies—until it suddenly stops. He looks down to find Ranger standing by his side.

"Good dog," Jacob said while he pets him. "Did you hear that, too?" he asked rhetorically.

* * *

Inside the garage, after finding and installing the few parts needed to start the engine of the 1957 Chevrolet, Jacob becomes increasing frustrated that the car will still not start. The engine cranks, but it refuses to turn over.

"C'mon, for fuck sake! Let's go!" Jacob told the car as he pounds the steering wheel.

While under the hood inspecting the carburetor, he hears a scratching sound coming from underneath the car. He stands straight and freezes. He then bends forward slightly to look around the fender and, as he does so, a highly agitated raccoon lunges for him. It laches on to his face and tears into his cheek. Jacob grabs hold of it in an attempt to throw the creature off. But, as he does, his flesh is pulled back like an orange peel. Blood flows from the wound. Just before Jacob takes it by the back of the neck, it drops to the ground, runs out of the garage and quickly climbs up a tree. Gone.

FRANCIS JOHN BALDUCCI

Chapter Five

Jacob toils in the basement, moving boxes and searching for winter clothes stored since the move. He notices blood droplets on the floor only to realize that the bandage on his cheek is soaked. He stares at his bloodied fingers after touching the wound and, as he does, he hears a crying baby upstairs. He asks himself whether the sound is truly coming from inside the house. As he turns toward the door, the sound stops. He then takes a deep breath and resumes his work.

While looking in a yellowed cardboard box, Jacob finds some of Katherine's old photographs. In her baby pictures, he sees her wear a broad smile while being bathed. He also finds pictures of Mitsy as a kitten; even then, the cat expressed evil. Near the bottom of the box, he finds pictures of her former boyfriend, Colton Vandenberg.

Colton went to the same school as Jacob and Katherine did and, like them, he was a business major. At the current time, he is not quite thirty years old. He is employed as a top executive at Whittendam Investments. Shortly after obtaining his position, and during a vacation in Europe, he met a young, attractive woman. Although his friends may say that Colton met the woman of his dreams, secretly, he never stopped loving Katherine. Nevertheless, he married the young woman after a year-long courtship. Perhaps he was captivated by her long, flowing blonde hair.

While Jacob continues to look at a few more photographs, he finds one of Colton and his young wife. Jacob saw this image before and thought nothing of it until his immediate epiphany—this woman's head is buried in the garden.

He tucks both the photograph inside the box and the idea deep inside his mind.

* * *

At the Clarkes' reception while Bill and Jacob spoke in private, Lorenzo invited the Donegals to his house for dinner and cards. This night had arrived, and Katherine experiences a little more positive excitement than usual.

Lorenzo's home is rather lush, and because he is a home-improvement expert, it contains many state-of-the-art furnishings and appliances. Lorenzo happily invites Jacob and Katherine into the main parlor where Shelby stands waiting. She wears a fitted turtleneck and a demure smile.

"Hello," she said.

"My, God!" Lorenzo said to Jacob; "what happened to your face?"

"Oh, I had an accident in the garage," Jacob answers. "It's just a scratch. There's no cause for concern."

"Okay, well, let's have a seat," Lorenzo said. "I made the eggplant puffs myself."

A silver tray of morsels sits on the Spanish coffee table. While they sit, Lorenzo gestures to the girl.

"Shelby can't even cook water," Lorenzo said in jest and laughs.

The demure smile leaves Shelby's lips. Katherine struggles to hold on to her grin.

"So...," Lorenzo said while everyone started chewing; "Jacob, do you hunt?"

"Yeah, I was meaning to ask you about all the animals in the room," Jacob said referring to the taxidermy trophies surrounding them of deer, boar, and black bear.

"Do you have raccoon?" Jacob asked.

"The hors d'oeuvres are quite good," Katherine interrupted.

"No, I don't hunt," Jacob finally answered.

"Oh, well, it's a lot of fun. You should go with me sometime. I use a bow—Here, let me show you."

Lorenzo retrieves a top-of-the-line compound bow from a nearby cabinet.

"Here, look at this beauty," Lorenzo said with pride: "It's the Bowtech Insanity. Here are the arrows: Easton Bloodline carbon with razor-sharp, dual-blade broadhead tips. It can reach a speed of 350 feet per second. It's powerful enough to take down a water buffalo."

"Good to know if I ever encounter one," Jacob said sarcastically.

Although Jacob was not trying to be humorous, he looks up to see Shelby laugh. He smiles back at her. The descriptions are not interesting to him, and the trophies are making him feel ill. When he looks into Shelby's eyes, he detects empathy.

"What about classic cars?" Lorenzo asked sensing Jacob's disinterest in hunting.

"I have one of those: a '57 Chevy Bel Air."

"No way! Gee, I would love to ride in one of those," Lorenzo said.

"Well, I can't seem to get it started. So, that might take some time. Hey, Shelby is a hot rod."

"My girlfriend, pal?" Lorenzo asked in a serious tone.

"No, the car—the Mustang Shelby," Jacob specified; "although, that is an interesting name," he said to her.

"Thank you," Shelby said.

"I'm sorry, folks," Lorenzo said with some embarrassment; "I jumped to conclusions a little. I can be a little bit insecure at times, but I'm working on it. Ain't that right, honey?" he said to Shelby.

She nods slightly.

"But, my girl is hot, right?" Lorenzo said with a giggle.

Shelby becomes slightly embarrassed and looks down. The room is suddenly silent.

"Maybe it's best that we eat now," Katherine suggested.

* * *

The dining table of rich cherry wood boasts fine china, crystal stemware, and linen. Lorenzo seems to have an enthusiasm—and especially the money—for the finer things. In the center of it all, a roast beef sits on a silver platter.

"Everything looks so delicious," Katherine said while she places a napkin over her lap.

"Thank you," Lorenzo said; "I learned everything about cooking from my nonna, God rest her soul. Please, everyone, *mangiamo*."

While the food is being passed about, and as mouths begin to fill, Jacob notices the trophy of an entire black bear in the room. Frozen in a menacing stance, its eyes seem to be fixed on him.

"So, tell me about the work that you've done to your home," Katherine asked.

"All the wood paneling that you see is all my doing," he said. "It adds richness to the room."

"What about the bear?" Jacob asked. "Did you kill it?"

Before Katherine could say anything, Lorenzo answers.

"Yes, I did. It took two arrows in the belly before it keeled over."

"How long have you lived here?" Katherine asked.

"Two years. The place was in rough shape—so much needed to be done."

"When did the two of you meet?" Jacob asked while looking at Shelby.

"Well, I threw a party here last year—a big one. A friend of mine brought her over to introduce us."

"So, it was an arranged meeting of sorts?" Jacob said.

"Yeah, and she never left," Lorenzo said with a smile.

"She dare not leave," Jacob said in jest while looking at the beef blood in his plate. Shelby tries to hold back a laugh. Lorenzo bears a puzzled look.

"Lorenzo, you should write a cookbook," Katherine said to distract.

"It's funny that you mention it; I was thinking about putting together a cookbook for wild game."

"Ah, yes: 'opossum parmesan'. Sounds delish," Jacob said sarcastically.

This time, Shelby laughs loudly. Lorenzo is visibly displeased with Shelby. Katherine notices the way Jacob looks at Shelby, but quickly dismisses any sort of tacit flirtation.

"Take my plate," Lorenzo orders Shelby. She removes both her plate and Lorenzo's plate to the kitchen.

"I can help you with the dishes," Katherine said to Shelby as she leaves the room.

"No, let her clean up. She likes cleaning up," Lorenzo advised. "It's the only thing she's good at."

Jacob and Katherine look at each other.

"Hey, let's play cards," Lorenzo said.

"Actually, it's getting kind of late," Jacob said; "and we're a bit tired. Next time."

As the Donegals put on their coats, Lorenzo volunteers his services to help them reconstruct their house.

"I'll do whatever work at a discount—a family discount."

"Thank you, Lorenzo," Katherine said; "that's sweet of you to offer."

* * *

As Katherine and Jacob make their way home, snow begins to fall heavily. All Jacob could think about was his next injection. After their arrival, Katherine makes a pot of tea.

"I'm going out for some firewood," Jacob said.

"Bring some back for the bedroom fireplace. That room is always cold."

Jacob enters the garage, sits in the Chevrolet, and opens the glove compartment. There, he retrieves the case that Randall gave him. He prepares a fix and injects himself. His body shakes. He breathes deeply.

After he composes himself, he reaches down in the corner of the garage to pick up some logs. He suddenly feels the small claws tear into his hand. Before he has time to react, a raccoon is ferociously assaulting him. Then, another. Then, a third. He picks up a log and swings it wildly. He strikes one, but the others attack with increased savagery. He swings so hard that it knocks one into a wall. He finds an opportunity to leave the garage and shut the door. As he takes a breath and inspects his wounds, with a blood-drenched log in his hand, he hears a deep growl. Without looking around, he begins to walk carefully toward the house. The growls become louder with each step that he takes. He then feels the impact on his back, which delivers him to the ground. Looking up, he sees a black bear, red-eyed, and poised for another strike. Jacob grabs the log, quickly stands, and bashes it on the side of its head. It startles the beast long enough for Jacob to make a desperate dash. He arrives inside the house and immediately shuts the door. While he quickly looks through the peep hole, he no longer sees the animal. Ranger barks at the door. Jacob then drops the log on the floor.

"We've got firewood!" he announced.

Chapter Six

Katherine is unaware of Jacob's growing addiction to methamphetamine. He has been increasing his use of the drug to the extent that he has developed skins rashes. Also, he shows signs of increased short-temperedness with her about the smallest of matters; on one occasion, Jacob abruptly snarled at her when she mentioned concern over his growing obsession with raccoons. It is evident to her that he has become so unhinged that he plots to kill every raccoon in the yard, and he recruits Ranger to assist him. Although the dog is loyal and enthusiastic to please his master, the raccoon time and time again prove to be too quick for the able and agile canine. The wound on Jacob's cheek healed well enough for him to remove the bandage. However, his hand is thoroughly wrapped as a result of his latest encounter with the prodigious procyon.

There is something else—something that distracts Jacob with increasing intrigue: Shelby. He imagines her brown, almond-shaped eyes, child-like facial features, olive skin complexion and dark hair. Her shape is exotic and soft. What began as a mere diversion has evolved into something more. He envisions enveloping her full, heart-shaped lips in a deep kiss. He fantasizes caressing and lifting her curved buttocks while taking her ample breasts into his mouth. Then, reality interrupts: he considers that this will never happen.

While in the yard, Jacob sharpens an ax. He plans on chopping wood; albeit, he also considers using the implement as a weapon against the other forms of nature that surround him.

"Jacob!" Lorenzo shouted from over a fence. "How ya' doin'? Ya' busy?"

"Yeah, but come over," Jacob said. "I'm just doing a little housekeeping." By this time, the ax is nearly razor-sharp.

"You're sharpening that ax?" Lorenzo asked.

"Yes, of course," Jacob answered.

"You don't need to sharpen it so much; it's a splitting ax. It's meant to be dull."

Jacob was unprepared for Lorenzo's insight.

"Well, then how does it cut?" Jacob asked.

"By the weight in the blade and the force of the swing."

"But, it wouldn't hurt if it's real sharp."

"Yeah, but it's not necessary," Lorenzo said gently. "Anyway, how are things? Shelby says hi. We had a great time, right?"

"Yes, good food. Which reminds me: Katherine and I will host a dinner party on Saturday evening.

She's having her friends over. You and Shelby are welcome to join us."

"Oh, great! We'll be there. We'll bring something."

"Okay. Just be certain to bring Shelby," Jacob insisted.

"You like her."

"Let me just say that she's a rare woman."

"I'll take that as a complement," Lorenzo said with a grin.

"Maybe you should."

* * *

The Donegals' dinner party is rather loud and festive. Most of the attendees consist of Katherine's old college friends. It had been seven years since they congregated together in dormitory rooms, smoking marijuana, and talking about the men that they were dating. The current gathering has brought out their younger selves. As it was then, they remotely know Jacob—even though some of them did attend their wedding.

Lorenzo and Shelby are also in attendance. They arrived somewhat later and managed to settle into a dim corner of the parlor.

Katherine spends much of her time with her friends. One friend in particular is named Cassie. She has a personality that is as colorful as the clothes that she wears. In fact, the loud laughing that you hear is coming from her.

Jacob, in the meantime, hovers around shuttling drinks and finger food. But, he does manage to keep an eye on Shelby. One moment, Jacob realizes that Lorenzo left her alone. Jacob walks over to her.

"Pigs in a blanket?" he asked.

"Oh, thank you. Is that honey Dijon?"

"Yes, it is; I made it myself," Jacob said with playful pride. "Are you having a good time?"

"Yes, I am," she answered with a smile. "Everyone seems to be very nice."

"How can you tell; you haven't moved around much."

"Oh, but I can tell." She points with her pinky while holding a morsel. "That woman over there in the tie-dye blouse—I'm having fun just watching her."

"Oh, yes. That's Cassie. She'll read your palm if you let her. She's sort of an amateur medium. She'll tell you all of your dreams and aspirations—all of your hopes."

"What do you mean?" Shelby asked almost rhetorically.

"Lorenzo makes you happy?" Jacob asked, hoping not to be too blunt.

"Let's just say he rescued me from destruction," she said while chewing.

"From a bad relationship? From drugs?"

She thinks. "From myself."

"So, it's love."

"Why are you so curious?" she asked playfully. "You think I could do better. Well, I can't."

"Sure you can."

"He provides for me," she insists.

"You're a kept woman. You're a prize."

"He cares about me; I don't need anyone but him."

"No friends?" Jacob smiles.

"I don't need anyone."

"*I* need you," he somewhat whispered in a lustful tone sensing that the moment is right.

Shelby reacts agape.

"I'm—," Jacob began.

"Jacob!" Lorenzo said, interrupting, as he rejoins Shelby; he puts his arm around her. "Nice place you have. I have some ideas for renovating it if you'd like to sit down sometime and discuss."

Shelby almost doesn't react to Lorenzo's return, but she does manage to offer Jacob a smile of appreciation for his candor.

"Sure, Lorenzo; that would be fine," Jacob said. "Excuse me, but I need to attend to the other guests."

As Jacob walks away, he realizes that he would have easily found love in Shelby, and that, perhaps, fate unjustly placed him in his current existence. With Shelby, there were no complications, no in-laws, no distractions, no obligations, no judging—just passion. He slowly looked back at her and noticed that she is still looking at him. She still expressed a sweet smile. He was glad that his comment did not make her feel uncomfortable.

* * *

At the dining table when the formal dinner concluded, the collective conversation reached a crescendo.

"Jacob, how are you doing?" Cassie asked from across the table. "This house is great, and so old. Any ghosts?"

"Well, if there are, you'll surely find them," Jacob retorted with a grin.

"No, seriously, let me conduct a séance here," Cassie said.

"I don't think so," Jacob said. "Let's leave the ghosts alone. Katherine and I don't want to be responsible for what happens," he added with a somewhat serious tone.

"Come on, Jacob," Katherine said. "It might be fun."

"Everybody, hold hands," Cassie directed. "C'mon, hold hands, everybody."

Everyone complies.

"Is there someone here from the other side?" Cassie began.

"I'm here at the other side," Lorenzo jokingly answered from the other side of the table. Cassie ignores him.

"Is there anyone here who would like to communicate with us from the great beyond? Anyone?"

Although Jacob has little confidence that Cassie knows what she is doing, he does secretly recall the strange sounds that he has been hearing in the house. If the house does indeed harbor some sort of entity, he hopes to himself that its presence is not detected by this gathering.

After a few minutes, it is apparent that Cassie is not detecting any sort of spiritual phenomena. Some guests appear restless in their seats while others laugh off the woman's fruitless attempts.

"Wait, I have something!" Cassie said with much excitement. She turns to a large leather bag in the corner of the room and from it she retrieves a Ouija board. Most guests express delight while others groan.

"Cassie, really?" Jacob asked.

"Oh, cool!" Katherine said. "Is that the same board we used to play with?"

"The same," Cassie answered.

"Well, break it out!" Katherine insisted.

Cassie lays the board on the table and places a wooden planchette on the board. A few participants around Cassie, including Katherine, place their fingertips on the planchette.

"Okay, let's ask some questions," Cassie said.

"Is there a spirit in the room with us?" Katherine asked.

The planchette immediately begins to move. It points to the first letter.

"C," Cassie said. "Someone write it down."

The next letter is selected.

"O," Katherine said.

The planchette slides to "L," and then "D." The planchette stops.

"Cold?" Cassie said. "The spirit's name is Cold?"

"Cold," Katherine confirmed.

"Okay, Cold, why are you here?" Cassie asked.

Again, the planchette immediately begins to move. It points to another letter.

"N," Katherine said. The planchette slides. "O—the next letter is O."

"Got it," Cassie said. The planchette slides again.

"S," Katherine said. It slides again. "E." The planchette stops.

"The answer is 'nose'? That doesn't make sense," Katherine said. "Cold nose."

"Maybe the spirit has a message for the dog," Cassie said jokingly.

Jacob stands visibly upset.

"That's enough!" he said. He picks up the planchette and throws it against the wall splintering it. "This party is quite fucking over."

* * *

The next morning, Jacob awoke with a raging headache. Katherine already got up and is downstairs. As he rolled out of bed, the rashes on his arms become more noticeable. He considered creams to cover them. He also considered using the veins in his foot. He did not consider stopping.

As he walked down the stairs, he accidentally stepped on Mitsy's tail. The cat let out a loud scream and scurried off into the shadows. He chuckled at the mishap.

Jacob made his way to the kitchen where Katherine was standing by a window looking out. He enters.

"What is wrong with you?" she asked.

"What?" he said while pouring a cup of coffee.

"You embarrassed me in front of my friends."

"I enlightened them."

"It was just an innocent board game—no different than Monopoly."

"Interesting comparison," he said while sipping.

"I mean it, Jacob!" she cried.

A howl is heard from the parlor.

"Ranger?" Jacob called out. "Here, boy!"

Jacob puts down his mug and hurries to the parlor. He sees the dog whimpering with bloody scratches on his nose. The front door is wide open. Before Jacob reaches the dog, it runs outside. Jacob takes chase. The dog continues to run fast, panic-stricken, down to the main road. Jacob loses sight of him. He hears tires screech and a loud thud. By the time he passes a clearing, he sees the dog lying on the side of the road, twisted, jerking, and bleeding profusely. After he approaches the animal, he kneels down and holds its head in his hands. The dog looks into Jacob's eyes, opens his mouth, and becomes still. Gone.

"It just jumped out from nowhere!" Jim the postman said.

"From nowhere?" Jacob returned.

Jacob looks down at his bloodied hands. Blood droplets form under him. He then looks at the battered frontend of the postal truck.

"I am so sorry, Mr. Donegal," Jim said.

Jacob takes Jim by his throat and slams him against the truck.

"How fast were you driving?" Jacob demanded.

"Sir, it's the main road," Jim insisted. "Why did your dog run out like that?"

Jacob appears to ignore the question and slowly releases him. He then carefully picks up the dog. He carries it to the house. Katherine stands below the veranda.

"Why did you leave the door open?" Jacob asked.

Katherine has a look of horror on her face.

"I didn't," she insisted.

Chapter Seven

It is an atypically frigid April. Frost forms around the windows outside of the master bedroom. Inside, Jacob experiences an early morning dream like no other. There, he is standing in an unfamiliar place. Shelby slowly appears before him. She stands naked and beautiful. Her hair gently moves, but there is no wind. She smiles and walks toward him. She is close enough for him to see her moist lips and how they join to beckon him for a gentle kiss. He obliges them with his eyes wide open. He then shivers as the cold bedroom air penetrates his dream. Shelby vanishes. Deep within a foggy abyss, Jacob hears a baby's cries. As he squints, shadowy images seem to manifest themselves but remain elusive. Materializing, a pale woman in black stands inches away from him. Her eyes appear as two empty holes. As he conveys a look of sympathy, she tightly grabs hold of both of his arms. Pain runs through his body from her. He then realizes the lucidity of his nightmare and struggles to regain consciousness. But, the mysterious woman refuses to let him go. Her mouth opens, and her teeth are gradually exposed as her face melts away. Jacob desperately tries to scream, but he cannot utter a sound. When he finally manages to free one arm, he finds himself twisted in the bed sheets. He turns toward Katherine, but she has already risen.

In the shower, Jacob thinks of his dream turned nightmare. He thinks of Shelby and how much he wants her. He then thinks of the pathetic woman and wonders who she is or who she represents. His thinking returns to Shelby, her body, and her mouth.

As Jacob enters the kitchen, he notices the morning news broadcast on the television. As he pours his coffee, his hands tremble slightly. The broadcast conveys IndustryOne Capital's announcement of the mass factory layoffs of Excelsior Manufacturing Company; they close their doors today.

Jacob has committed himself to the ways of corporate greed and the destruction in its wake. He knows this all too well and, because of this, he dreads the drive to his office.

With every passing mile in his car, he feels the tension rising. However, he will go along with the plans of IndustryOne and resist resignation.

* * *

Although the suites buzz with activity over the takeover of Excelsior, Jacob sits quietly at his desk. Randall is on vacation and is presumably engaging in some sort of acts of debauchery and indulgence. So, Jacob's current existence is free of comic relief. His day is relatively uneventful right up until he packs his attaché case and heads down to the building garage.

As Jacob enters the garage and walks toward his car, he does not see the garage attendant as he normally does. Jacob gets into his car and drives off.

Before Jacob leaves the city limits, Bill Clarke suddenly emerges from the backseat and produces a pistol. He places it to Jacob's head.

"Keep driving!" Bill demanded.

"What are you doing?"

"Just keep driving, and shut up!"

Jacob continues to drive, down streets and side streets, until he reaches a secluded location within an abandoned construction site.

"Okay, stop here," Bill said. Jacob complies.

Both men get out of the car and, with Bill behind Jacob pressing the pistol against his back, they walk a few paces to a clearing.

"Now, turn around," Bill demanded. Jacob turns to see Bill a few feet away pointing the pistol towards Jacob's chest. Jacob raises his hands slowly.

"My life is ruined because of you," Bill said slowly.

"You've got it all wrong, Bill," Jacob responded with a slight tremor in his voice.

"...and now I'm going to kill you."

Jacob sees Bill's pistol hand shaking.

"You don't want to do this," Jacob pleads. "My wife, do you remember my wife? She's expecting a baby. We're expecting a baby. Do you hear me? A baby, you fuck!"

Bill, realizing what he is doing, places the pistol muzzle into his mouth and pulls the trigger. The pistol blows a bloody halo of brain matter from the back of his head. His body immediately drops to the ground. Jacob's body jolts, but he quickly regains some of his composure. With his hands still raised, he walks to the crumpled body to inspect it. Gone.

* * *

It is the following day, and Jacob is at home in his garage breathing in deeply after having just injected himself. He sits in the backseat of the Chevrolet. He considers working on the classic car to take his mind off of the terror that he has experienced. However, he did not want to add frustration to his predicament because he still cannot get the engine started. While sitting there, he thinks of simpler times. He thinks of unbridled fun.

"Is anyone here?" she said in a soft voice.

Jacob quickly hides his meth case.

"I'm here! Who is it?" Jacob responded.

"It's me, Shelby."

"Oh, Shelby! C'mon in!"

Jacob gets out of the car. While doing so, Shelby steps inside of the garage.

"How are you?" Jacob asked. Shelby unsuccessfully attempts to conceal a small bruise on her cheek with a lock of her hair. "What happened?" Jacob said while noticing the bruise.

"It's nothing."

"Tell me," Jacob insists. "Did Lorenzo do that? Did he hit you?" He moves closer to her.

"He didn't mean to; I could be impossible sometimes," she declared.

"That's nonsense!—No man should ever lay his hand on a woman."

Shelby moves closer to Jacob.

"Please hold me," she asked in a tender voice.

Jacob carefully puts his arms around her. She exhales. He gently maneuvers his mouth to hers and kisses her. For a moment, he is in disbelief. She, nonetheless, had this encounter somewhat planned.

Jacob draws her body deeper into the garage. He kisses her again—this time, with increased intensity and passion. Her body becomes slightly limp. He turns her around, and caresses her round, well-shaped buttocks. Both of them begin to breathe heavily. He begins grinding her for a few moments, bending her over the car hood, before pulling down her pants and spreading her legs. He removes his sizable erection from his pants and inserts it into her. The sex is brutal, unlike what the both of them ever imagined. He is hurting her: thrusting hard, twisting her arms, and grabbing her hair and pulling it tightly. He then begins slapping her in the face, violently and repeatedly. She is in distress, but she dares not break away.

"Are you okay, Jacob?" Katherine called out from the kitchen window, not aware of Shelby's presence. Jacob stops.

"I'm fine. I'm just working out a little before lunch," Jacob answered while out of breath. He pulls Shelby up and tells her to be quiet. As they regain their proper appearances, they hear Katherine enter the rear yard. Jacob steps out of the garage with an announcement.

"Look who stopped by: it's Shelby," Jacob declared while gesturing to her. Shelby steps out.

"Hi," she said.

"Oh, my! What happened to your face?" Katherine asked with concern.

"Lorenzo assaulted her," Jacob insisted.

"My goodness, your face is all bruised," Katherine said.

Just as Katherine spoke, a trickle of blood emerged from one of Shelby's nostrils.

"Come inside the house and let my help you," Katherine urged. Droplets of blood appear on the brickwork at Shelby's feet.

"No, I'm fine; I don't want to impose," Shelby pleads. "I sort of panicked and came here, but I'm feeling better now. I have to go."

Shelby quickly leaves while Katherine stands dumbfounded. Jacob turns to Katherine with a question.

"Well, what's for lunch?"

* * *

The local weather reports indicate that a powerful storm is headed toward the small New England town and its surrounding areas. It is estimated that this storm will be the worst in thirty years and that residents should take its wrath very seriously. So, Jacob labors to board up some of the windows, store some items indoors and in the garage, and secure any loose items to the ground. He then thinks of Mitsy. The cat is occasionally let outdoors; tonight should be no exception, he thinks. After whispering for her outside in a mock call, he smiles and goes inside.

Chapter Eight

In the aftermath of the storm, Jacob surveys the property to assess any damage. Under a loose board near the garden gate, he sees green, glowing eyes. After he quickly lifts the board, he learns that Mitsy is still alive. As he calls to it, the creature savagely attacks him. Its claws dig deeply into his face. He feels his blood run down his cheek as he struggles to pry her away. He finally removes the animal and quickly impales it on the spear-like points of the garden gate. After a few moments, it stops struggling.

* * *

While Jacob is in the bathroom washing the blood from his face and hands, he hears Katherine rise.

"How is it outside?" she asked from behind the door.

"Pretty bad, but I'll get to work fixing things," he answered.

"Have you seen Mitsy?" she asked after a short pause.

"No, I think she is somewhere in the house. Maybe the storm spooked her." Jacob then dresses the wounds on his face. Luckily, he has not shaved in some time, and the growth somewhat covers his injuries.

"Coffee?" she asked.

"Sure, thanks."

Katherine goes downstairs to the kitchen while Jacob presses gauze tightly against his face.

As Jacob walks down the stairs, he hears Katherine scream.

"My, God! Mitsy!"

"What? What is it?" Jacob asked.

Jacob sees Katherine staring out of the kitchen window into the rear yard. They both go outside to see the pathetic, impaled pet.

"What happened to my Mitsy?" Katherine cried.

"Maybe she got picked up by the strong winds," Jacob said with weak certainty.

"Is that possible?"

"Sure it is."

"Why was she left out last night?"

"I thought she came in," Jacob asserted.

"My poor thing!" Katherine cries and is barely consolable.

"Let's go back inside. I'll give her a proper burial in the corner of the garden. Okay?"

Jacob walks Katherine back into the house. He then reemerges with a garbage bag.

* * *

The Waterside Pub is a local bar that caught Jacob's attention a few times while he was running errands. On this evening, he decided to stop in to quench his thirst. As he drove into the parking lot, he was not expecting much. He merely wanted to have a few drinks and unwind.

While Jacob enters the establishment, he is struck with the strong smell of sour beer and onion soup. The interior is so old that the piping for the original gaslight fixtures remains on the walls. A framed black-and-white print of Franklin Pierce hangs prominently over the fireplace. Jacob finds an empty stool at the bar and sits on it. He is next to two older men having a lively discussion. He takes a careful look and sees no concern to sit near them. So, he decides to stay put.

Directly in front of where he sits, he sees an attractive woman nursing a beer. Even under the dimly-lit room, he clearly sees that she put her makeup on wrong. To his left, he sees a nervous-looking businessman in a crumpled suit shaking his tumble. In the corner, he sees an old couple gently dancing to a progressive British-rock song over a low-volume jukebox.

"What can I get you?" the bartender asked.

"Glenfiddich, if you got," Jacob answered.

"We got."

After a few moments, Jacob's attention turns back to the two men. One of them tries to bring Jacob into the conversation, but Jacob is reluctant to join in.

"My friend here says that cops should be the only ones carrying guns. What do you think?" the man asked Jacob.

"I don't know," Jacob responded while his drink arrives; "I try not to think." He turns his attention to the attractive woman and considers sitting next to her.

"Where do you live, fella?" the other man asked Jacob.

"I live on Oaks." Jacob throws back his drink and gestures for another.

"Which one? My name is Brian, by the way." Brian extends his hand.

"The one at the end." Jacob shakes Brian's hand halfheartedly.

"Carl," the other man said.

"At the end?" Brian asked. "Seven?"

"Yeah."

"That's the Cole house," Carl said.

"Yes, the Cole house," Jacob said.

"You've heard of the Coles?" Brian asked.

"Not really," Jacob answered.

"You bought their house and you haven't heard of them?" Brian asked with surprise.

"It's the murder house," Carl said.

"What?" Jacob turns toward them.

"Thomas Cole killed his wife, Adeline, in that house," Brian said.

"More like Tom Cole savagely mutilated his wife by throwing acid into her face," Carl said. "He then built a structure to house her disfigured body. He went so mad that he eventually cut her to pieces and strangled their baby boy before killing himself."

"Much of this is not fully known," Brian interrupted. "You don't know any of this?" he asked Jacob.

"I have to go," Jacob said hastily. He throws money on the bar and walks out without saying another word. He leaves his drink.

* * *

It is the next morning, and Jacob had a sleepless night. He decides to visit the local library to research the Coles. He is deeply compelled to find out the truth.

After consulting with a librarian and after reading some digitized news articles, he confirms much of the information that the bar patrons told him. The stories convey that Thomas Cole was a cold-hearted killer who committed suicide. He reads a quote from Chief Johnston that creates more questions than answers.

Jacob then thinks of Bob Lewis. He recognizes that there was no disclosure to him concerning the murders. Also, he learns that disclosure laws are not well-defined and that they are under-enforced. Jacob realizes that it was no wonder that the house stayed off the market and was uninhabited for three years until he purchased it. Otherwise, the house may never have been purchased right away. Jacob wants answers.

Chapter Nine

Thomas and Adeline Cole were newly-wedded when they arrive at Seven Oaks. After Thomas acquired estate monies upon his father's passing, which also included the acquisition of a 1957 Chevrolet, and after their modest wedding ceremony, the innocent pair pulls into the long driveway with the anticipation of having children and living long, cherished lives.

Their classic car gleams with as much youth and vitality as the Coles. They rush up the steps to the great front door and open it with similar haste. The home is splendid but empty and in need of repair and renovation. Conveniently, Thomas is a talented builder and carpenter by trade.

Almost without hesitation and with much enthusiasm, he begins specific work on the house replacing double-hung windows, reinforcing corner brackets, and re-mortaring the variably-patterned base brickwork among other tasks.

Adeline is feminine and delicate in form and regarded by her husband as the "salt of the earth." She is impeccable and competent in everything that she does, and she easily takes to her role as housekeeper. Keeping a clean house, to her, is an important way to convey her love to her husband. Spring arrived, and she anticipates that she will spend much of her time in the garden growing flowers and vegetables to sit on the kitchen table—a piece of furniture that Thomas regards as his "personal work in progress." It doesn't matter to Adeline that it wobbles a little; it was made by the hands of the man that she loves, and that is all that matters to her.

Before the weather dampens, Thomas hastily plans to build a structure on the property for utility purposes and to store the car. He chooses a location not far from the back door on top of an existing foundation from a former structure. As he toils, Adeline makes fresh lemonade and brings it to him. He repays her efforts with kisses and loving glances. Throughout this project, he openly laments that he never took her on an appropriate honeymoon. She insists that the glorious honeymoon never ended.

* * *

Upon completion of the modest, sturdy structure, the car and several tools enter their new home. Its only entrance is a well-constructed garage door. Thomas jokes that he may need the place overnight if he ever upset Adeline. She playfully and softly threatens to take him up on the offer.

* * *

Thomas and Adeline plan to have children. The thought had always been on their minds. Two months elapsed, four months, and then eight months and still no conception. The more time that passes with no good fortune, the more anxious they become. They deeply believe that children would serve as a product of their love. They increasingly become obsessed, but they remain optimistic.

Even after they attempt for an entire year to conceive at least one child, they refuse to believe that they may be incapable. Thomas may regard the endeavor as laborious if he did not take pleasure in loving Adeline's beautiful form.

* * *

It is the season of severe rain to their area. The ground is thoroughly muddied after a serious downfall from the night before. While Thomas is in town getting supplies, Adeline accesses the status of her garden. She is surprised to find considerable water damage. As she walks inside the garden, she notices that all the flowers are crushed; the vegetables are inedible. With some disappointment, she realizes that she will need to start over.

After Adeline dropped a handful of her lifeless harvest, she makes her exit toward the garden gate. She takes only a few steps on the slippery ground before she loses her footing. While trying to break her fall, she outstretches her arms—almost as though she attempts to take flight. However, she falls hard—

cutting her face on the gate's spear-like points. The injury is not as extensive as it could be because her hands absorbed much of the fall. Yet, she knows that she needs to treat the wound quickly. If she washes the blood off and dresses the injury, it might not alarm Thomas as much when he arrives home, she thinks.

* * *

"What happened?" Thomas said. "Take the bandage off and let me see."

"No! It's nothing. I fell in the yard. It's only a scratch."

"Let me see."

Adeline allows Thomas to peel back the bandage revealing an abrasion wound severe enough to tear open a small area of her cheek. Blood tricks from it as Thomas inspects.

"We have to go to the doctor," he insisted.

* * *

A few hours later, Adeline is resting comfortably at home. She was prescribed a topical remedy and ten small pills to take every twelve hours.

Thomas inspects the gate. He discovers that it is rusted and bacteria-ridden. Albeit, he is confident that the medicine will prevent an infection.

As he nurses her, she protests.

"Don't fuss over me. Go build something," she said somewhat playfully. He reluctantly takes her advice.

One week later, the wound worsens. It is infected and it nearly doubles in size. Adeline keeps this to herself. She thinks it will heal after the pills take effect. She does not want to worry Thomas, she thinks, unnecessarily.

* * *

A bandage remained on Adeline's face for over two weeks. Thomas thinks he minimized his involvement long enough.

"Is the wound any better? And, why a bigger bandage?"

"It's getting better," she said, brushing off his concern. But, as she increasingly remains in denial, Adeline's body continues to betray her.

"Let me see." As Thomas inspects the wound, it is evident to him that the medicine has not been effective. What he sees is a horrific sight that occupies nearly half of her cheek. The wound is composed of white and red blotches saturated with puss. It is very infected and it appears to be spreading slowly downward. The smell is rotten and pungent.

"We need to go back to the doctor. Something went wrong," he said with desperation. Adeline, however, remains calm.

* * *

It has been eight months since the accident and Adeline's condition has become dire. Even after several doctor's visits and aggressive medicines, the wound spread to her entire cheek and part of her neck. Operations to repair some of her injuries failed. With her mouth gone, Adeline now garbled. Yet, Thomas fully understands her. It is helpful that much of her communication involves points, gestures, and occasionally, scribbled words on a small notepad.

Throughout the entire affliction, Thomas becomes increasingly consumed with grief and guilt. He works tirelessly to nurse her back. Admittedly, it is resolved by the doctor that she will soon die and that the only thing left to do is to keep her comfortable.

* * *

An entire year passes. A small amount of skin remains on her face and neck. Bone and blood vessels are exposed. Saliva steadily drips from her bone-white chin. Puss slowly flows from crevices in between the muscles. There is never enough gauze or small towels available to absorb the fluids. Matters have become so desperate that Adeline makes Thomas promise to never remove her from their home and to never accept visitors.

Despite Adeline's failing health and because of her dire circumstances, they both decide to quickly resume their attempts at conceiving a child. This plan comes about in large part by Thomas's insisting. Only the product of their love, he thinks, would allow some part of Adeline to live on. They determined the day of her ovulation. On their bed, she would lay on her back as still as possible with towels under her head and neck and a cloth covering her face. Thomas would carefully mount her. When the time arrived, they got started.

The pace is slow, at first. The rotted smell makes it difficult for Thomas to prolong his erection. As he thrusts more aggressively, the cloth covering her face unexpectedly drops to the floor revealing Adeline's grotesqueness. He notices her flowing tears intermingling with an increasing amount of puss in between the bacteria-eaten crevices of her raw face. Rather than reach for the cloth to cover the sight, he shuts his eyes tightly and concentrates—making certain to convey his contents deep inside of her.

"I love you," he whispered in her ear hole when he was done.

* * *

Adeline carried to full term and is within hours of giving birth. Thomas, meanwhile, is preparing at a medium pace. There is little concern that the child was infected by its mother; much of the infection did not travel downward from the neck. They are anticipating a healthy child.

She is positioned comfortably on the bed. Thomas goes through the checklist in his mind.

"Shhizz-chaa," she said. "Kkrugg."

"Names," he replied. "I know, at birth."

"[Okay]," she said.

As he speaks with her, he notices a small trace of blood on the sheet that covers her lap. When he lifts it, he sees a sizable puddle. She severely hemorrhaged without ever knowing it.

"We have to get it out! Can you push?"

"[Take the knife]!" she screamed. "[It's dying]!"

"Wha—?"

"[Use it]! [Here, cut here]," she showed him. "[Now]!"

Confident that the blade is well sterilized, he steadily incises her entire lower abdomen. After a swell of blood subsided, he reaches in for the child. It is moving. He feels the feet, carefully pulls, and retrieves it. After wiping blood from the face, he looks upon him. Unfortunately, he has his mother's looks; Thomas quickly learns that the boy is severely mutilated by the disease. Thomas's gasp was interrupted by the boy's loud cry. He grabbed the blanket and immediately wraps his son. He cleans more blood from his face, looks deeply into the boy's eyes and smiles at him.

"David."

"[Yes]," she nodded.

After a brief moment, as she bled, eviscerated, Adeline expels her last breath. She never sees her son's face. She is spared the horror, Thomas thinks.

* * *

After an hour, David is near death. Thomas could do nothing but comfort him by singing over and over a lullaby he remembered from childhood. He sings it until David's tiny body becomes limp.

* * *

With both bodies thoroughly cleaned, he dresses Adeline, delicately, in burial clothes. He then folds the baby into her arms.

In the garden, he digs a deep grave for his family. When the hole is deep enough, he carefully lowers them in.

After the last shovel of earth is placed over their bodies, Thomas goes into the garage and retrieves a long rope.

While inside the house, he stares up at the exposed central beam. He imagines Adeline's smile; he anticipates that he will soon be reunited with her. After he secures the rope to the beam, he thinks of David. He envisions that he will soon play with him until they both laugh uncontrollably.

He stands high on a small table as he ties the noose. He tightens it around his neck, closes his eyes, and leaps.

As he feels the burning of the rope around his neck and while he experiences his body become lifeless, he feels Adeline embrace him. With David lovingly tucked under her arm, all are gone.

* * *

After nearly two months, a report from the local post office of a foul stench at the Cole house reaches Chief Johnston. There is also word of an accumulation of unopened mail at the front door. Seizing one of his deputies and the keys to his cruiser, he heads out to investigate.

* * *

While standing in the main parlor, they discover voluminous amounts of blood and other bodily fluids sloshed on the floors. The smell is unbearable to any veteran law enforcer. Above their heads dangles the noose.

"My, God! What happened here?" the deputy said.

"I don't know," Johnston thought aloud in his astonishment. "Check for victims," he directed after regaining some of his composure.

While the deputy quickly embarks on the search, Johnston has a premonition that this mystery may never be solved. He did not know why he feels this way. Somehow, he knows that this horrific encounter will continue to beleaguer him.

Chapter Ten

Jacob bursts into the police station and demands to see Chief Johnston. Just before the deputy subdues him, Johnston emerges from his office.

"That's okay, Wayne!" Johnston orders. "Let him in."

"Why did you *really* visit my house?" Jacob asked Johnston angrily while he passes through the railed divider gate. "Tell me why!"

"Come in my office," Johnston said calmly. He turns to the bewildered deputy. "Take messages; I don't want to be disturbed."

Both men enter the office. While Johnston closes the door, he gestures for Jacob to have a seat.

"So, you want to know why I paid you a visit," Johnston said. "I take it that you found out about the Coles."

"I did. What happened? What did you see?"

"It was among the most horrific sights my deputy and I have ever encountered. There was blood everywhere. I have never forgotten it."

"Why didn't you tell me?" Jacob asked.

"I didn't think you needed to know. I even thought that you may have already found out. I don't know. Coffee?"

"No, thank you. But, there had to be a reason for your visit. I read your quote from an article concerning the deaths. You said that you will always be 'haunted' by this case. Why haunted?"

Johnston takes in a deep breath before answering.

"Although I closed the investigation, I have not entirely dismissed the case."

"Why not?" Jacob asked.

Johnston takes a sip of his coffee and gulps audibly before answering.

"We never found any of the Cole bodies."

* * *

The Donegal baby is born on a humid mid-July morning. It is a healthy boy. Jacob names him David, only because he favors the name over any other. Jacob is uncertain who the child resembles. Thus far, his ears, eyes, skin tone, and hair color are neither his nor Katherine's. He leaves Katherine and David at the hospital and goes to the office.

As Jacob sits at his desk, he realizes that perhaps it would be best if they move from Seven Oaks. In the halls, he sees Randall a few times but, for whatever reason, his young friend seems a bit elusive and not himself. He senses that something is seriously wrong with the man. He calls his office and leaves a message.

"Randall, it's Jake. Can you come to my office, please?"

After nearly an hour, a knock comes to Jacob's door.

"It's open," Jacob said.

Randall hurries in and quickly takes a seat.

"Why have you been avoiding me, Randall?"

No sooner after Randall sits does he begin scratching his arms rigorously. Jacob notices.

"Randall, show me your arms."

"What?"

"Roll up your sleeves and show me your arms."

Randall complies.

"My, God!"

"Pretty gross, right?" Randall quipped.

Much of Randall's arms are covered in serious skin rashes encrusted with flakey scabs around the most infected areas.

"How long have you used?" Jacob asked.

"It's been some time now." Randall hesitates. "Um, I'm scared."

"What's wrong?"

"I can't stop shaking," Randall said in a serious tone.

Jacob stands, sits next to him and puts his arm around him.

"Jake, there's something I need to tell you."

"Go on."

"A few months ago, I saw your wife at a downtown café with another man. I'm sorry I didn't tell you sooner."

Jacob takes a deep breath.

"Describe him," Jacob asked calmly.

"Blonde, wavy hair, tall."

"Was he slim, with chiseled features?"

"Yes, and very well-dressed."

"Colton."

Randall starts to shake more intensely. It quickly becomes uncontrollable.

"Randall, you need help. I have to call you an ambulance."

"No, I'm fine. I just need to get back to my office to finish my work. I have a lot of numbers to crunch."

Just as Randall rises to his feet, he collapses to the carpet.

"Randall!" Jacob called out.

Jacob drops to check Randall's vital signs. He opens his collar and then grabs the phone to call 911. "Randall, you're going to be all right!" Jacob finds Randall's pulse. It is racing.

Moments later, as the ambulance arrives, Randall begins to convulse. Foam emerges from his mouth. The paramedics remove Randall on a stretcher with extreme haste.

After the commotion subsided, Jacob sits in one of the guest chairs. He tries to take in what he witnessed. His phone rings a number of times before he fully realizes it. He picks up.

"Donegal," he answered.

"Where the hell have you been?" Mr. Storch said.

"I'm sorry, sir. Did you hear about Randall?"

"Forget Randall! I want you in my office now." Mr. Storch hangs up.

Ordinarily, Jacob would be scared. He would think that his career is coming to an end. Even worse—that his life is over. But, not this time.

Mr. Storch's office door swings open so violently that it slams into the wall.

"You wanted to see me, sir?" Jacob said mockingly to Mr. Storch seated at his desk.

"See here, I needed that Excelsior disposition report a week ago. Frankly, Jacob, I'm surprised at you."

"I'm surprised myself—at a lot of things around here, sir," Jacob retorted.

"What are you talking about?" Mr. Storch demanded.

"IndustryOne doesn't build, it doesn't manufacture. It picks the flesh off of dying carcasses," Jacob said angrily.

"How dare you?"

"It destroys people's lives!"

"Maybe you should take the rest of the day off," Mr. Storch advised sternly.

"Maybe you should go fuck yourself," Jacob returned.

"Take the rest of the day off, Jacob!"

"And, maybe you should go fuck yourself."

"Well, I never thought I'd ever have to say this to you, Jacob, but, you're fired!" Mr. Storch picks up the phone. "Security, I want you to escort Mr. Donegal from the building. See to it immediately." He hangs up.

"I'll see you in hell, Steven! That's where I'll be waiting for you."

Jacob leaves.

* * *

Jacob decides to not yet inform Katherine of his termination. He considers holding out until he finds another job. The tension seems unbearable, and the addition of a baby adds to the pressure. He considers quitting meth, but he is in denial that he will never end up like Randall. He also reasons with himself that he needs the drug for better concentration.

Overshadowing any glimmer of hope are deep thoughts of despair. At times, he feels as if the world around him is falling apart and there is no place for him to turn. His outward signs of drug addiction are apparent, and he thinks that it is only a matter of time before Katherine begins to notice. His arms begin to scab. Insomnia occurs too often, and when he does manage to fall sleep, he has nightmares that are from bizarre to terrifying. Sometimes when he goes to bed, he wishes that he never wakes up. He thinks of Ranger often, and regards him as his only true friend. He thinks of reuniting with him.

At the town's coffee shop, Jacob sits staring down into a black cup. He purchased a newspaper, but he has not opened it; he merely read the front page and then turned his attention back to his coffee. Minutes later, a young woman enters and, after a slight hesitation, she sits next to Jacob. She is somewhat attractive with short, dark hair. Her perfume reaches his nose.

"Tea, please?" she asked the counterman.

The beverage is prepared with haste and is placed in front of her. She adds sugar and milk to the cup. As she stirs, she glances over to Jacob's newspaper.

"May I see your paper?" she asked Jacob politely.

"Sure," Jacob answered without looking at her. He moves it toward her.

"Thanks." She takes the newspaper and opens it. "There is so much crime in the city; you never know who you can trust," she said as she turns the pages.

"You got that right," Jacob returned.

"My name is Rachel," she said while seizing an opportunity. They make eye contact.

"Nice to meet you, Rachel. I'm Jacob."

"Nice to meet you, Jacob. Say, listen, I need a lift somewhere. I have no money—I barely have enough for the tea. Um, can you help me?"

Jacob thinks for a moment, and realizes that he has nothing better to do. He also considers that she is harmless and vulnerable.

"Sure, no problem. Do you want to leave now?"

"Yeah, just let me use the ladies' room. I'll be right out."

"Take your time," he said.

As she leaves the counter, Jacob looks her over. He thinks of groping her. He then stands, puts some money on the counter, and walks slowly toward the door. Rachel emerges.

"Ready," she said.

He smells a new application of perfume.

While in his car, they don't talk much. All that was discussed thus far was that she needs a ride a few towns over.

"Nice car," she said while moving her curvy body in the seat.

A few minutes into the trip, Jacob notices Rachel looking at him.

"What are you staring at?" Jacob said somewhat playfully.

"You're cute," she responded.

"Thanks." Jacob smiles.

"Say, you're not a cop, are you?"

"No, why?"

"Well, I was wondering, maybe I could do something for you if you do something for me."

"Like what?" Jacob's smile broadens.

"C'mon, you know what I mean," she said with a giggle.

"Okay, I'm game. How much?"

"Forty bucks."

"Forty bucks?"

"I'm real good. Bareback."

Jacob mimics thinking.

"Okay, forty bucks," he said.

Jacob finds a place to pull over. He shuts off the engine and headlights. He then unbuckles his pants and removes his penis.

"There are some tissues in the glove compartment," he instructed.

She takes a handful of tissues, leans down into his lap and goes to work. After a few minutes, the deed is done. She wipes her face rigorously to retrieve every drop.

"There, how was that?" she asked.

Jacob immediately punches her in the face. Blood shoots out of her nose. In a panic, she reaches for the door handle, but she struggles to see through her blood-filled eyes and is unable to find it. She finally opens the door only to find Jacob outside. He assails her more by repeatedly grabbing and punching her in the chest and back. She begins to plea for her life. He, contrarily, doesn't utter a word. After he kicked her a few times, he stops. He then takes out his wallet and removes some money.

"Here's your forty bucks," he said. He throws the money on her trembling body. "You're right; you are real good."

Jacob gets back into his car and drives off.

* * *

The Whittendam mansion is spacious and well-appointed. In the west den, Katherine and her baby visit with Constance. The two talk of various topics that lead them to Lloyd and Jacob.

"Mom, did dad ever display serious anxiety when I was born?" Katherine asked while holding David.

"Oh, yes," Constance answered with a smile. "He's always been a brilliant man, but when it came to you, he was clueless. He didn't even know how to hold you."

"The reason why I'm asking is because Jacob has been acting strange lately."

"Oh, give him time. He'll get adjusted. Things have a way of working themselves out." Constance hesitates for a moment. "Speaking of your father, he asked me why you named our grandson David."

"Jacob chose the name."

"Any reason why?"

"I don't know.   I think he said he likes the name."

"And, how do you feel about the name?"

"Mom, it's a nice name."

"Well, okay..."

"Mom, tell me."

"Your father thought it was a poor choice."

"Ah, please."

"He said that it's a 'Jew name'."

"Mom, please.   Dad's totally out of his mind," Katherine said while Constance ignores her quip.

"Let me have my grandson!" Constance said with her arms outstretched and wearing a wide smile. As soon as the baby is in her arms, she bombards him with kisses.

"Oh, I can just eat you up," Constance said.

* * *

Meanwhile, at the house, Jacob toils in the garden. Through the branches of a tall tree, he sees a raccoon. It appears to be stalking him. He pursues it as it drops down to the ground. They recognize one another. While he makes his way to the ground to prepare to pounce on it, he keeps a watchful eye on the splitting ax resting against the garage. As he looks up, he is confronted by Lorenzo carrying his compound bow. Strapped around him is a quiver of razor-sharp arrows.

"I knew I shouldn't have trusted you with Shelby!" Lorenzo said with extreme anger. He loads one of the arrows on to the bow.

"Wait a second, Lorenzo!" Jacob said while holding up his hands. "Don't do anything stupid."

The arrow strikes Jacob in the thigh.

"Arrggh!" Jacob screamed. "You fuck! What are you doing?"

"You fucked her, didn't you?" Lorenzo asked while grinding his teeth.

"Stop, just stop!" Jacob said while moving toward the ax. "Now, just calm down and we can talk about this."

"She left me, you know. She left me for good." Lorenzo said while loading another arrow.

"Because you're a fuck!"

Lorenzo fires shooting Jacob in the same leg, but the wound is not as deep as the first one inflicted. Out of desperation, and while Lorenzo takes a breath, Jacob obtains the ax and charges Lorenzo. Blood is pouring from Jacob's wounds, but he does not allow the pain to stop him. Lorenzo, caught unexpectedly, fails in his attempt to reload another arrow. Instead, it drops to the ground. At that moment, Jacob swings the ax striking Lorenzo across the chest. The force is so strong that the ax imbeds itself. Jacob falls to the ground and drags himself for a few feet. The blood pours from Lorenzo's wound. Bubbles then appear around the wound as air escapes from his lungs. He falls to his knees.

"God!" Lorenzo whispered before falling forward to the ground.

Jacob makes a feeble attempt to remove the arrows from his leg. The points are barbed, although he does manage to remove one of them; he breaks the imbedded arrow in half for the time being. He takes hold of Lorenzo's body and removes the ax. He drags the body into the garden, digs a hole as deep as he can under the circumstances, and quickly buries Lorenzo.

Jacob loses consciousness.

* * *

"My, God! Jacob! What happened?" Katherine cried when she came home to see Jacob bloodied and laying in the rear yard.

"I saw that fucking raccoon again," Jacob said in a weak voice. "I borrowed one of Lorenzo's bows with some arrows to try and shoot it. But, I tripped and stabbed myself."

"Let me help you into the house!"

With much of his weight on Katherine's shoulders, Jacob looks back to make certain that none of Lorenzo's limbs are protruding from the ground.

Chapter Eleven

It is September, and a year has elapsed since the Donegals moved in. Jacob has been walking with a cane ever since the injury he received from Lorenzo. Jacob did not see much of the police since his disappearance. It was presumed that Lorenzo somehow took his own life somewhere after Shelby left him.

Jacob has a more pressing issue that plagues him; he cannot remove from his mind what Randall told him regarding Katherine. The thought that Katherine has been secretly having an affair with Colton paralyses his body and mind. He considers when they may have initiated their liaison. He is uncertain whether or not it began since the purchase of the house. He wonders why she would go along with moving in with him if she considered reconciling with Colton. There is one thing he realizes that he must do: he must determine if David, who is now five months old, is truly his son. He must find out the truth by administering a paternity test.

After purchasing a small kit from the local pharmacy, and after mailing the swabbed samples and a fee to the laboratory address on the box, Jacob received the results within a week.

As he read the results, with his hands trembling, one of his most horrific imaginations has been realized.

The feeling of betrayal overcomes him to the extent that he can feel the blood fill up into his face. His fists tightly clench the report until it shreds into pieces in between his throbbing fingers.

* * *

While she is in the garden, Katherine hastily picks some flowers to use as a centerpiece for the dining table. She snips them carefully, and places them into a vase that her and Jacob received as a housewarming gift. Without her knowing it, Jacob was standing behind her after coming from upstairs.

"Gasp!" she uttered. "I didn't know you were there."

"Here I am, babe," he responded.

"Oh, good. I need you to watch the baby for a moment."

"Sure, no problem."

As she trots upstairs, Jacob approaches the baby sitting in his highchair. He strokes the baby's face. As he does so, the baby manages to bite down on one of Jacob's fingers. He bites down hard and his tiny teeth are sharp enough to tear into Jacob's skin.

Blood drips from the wound onto the kitchen counter and the floor. Jacob manages to hold in a scream. He takes a paper towel and wraps it around the wound and wipes up the blood. As soon as he is done, Katherine returns.

"Ah, I'm cooking tonight," Jacob declared. "It's our fourth wedding anniversary, and your parents will be over later, so I think I'll prepare something special."

"That's great, baby," Katherine said. "Later, I have to go to the hairdresser so I look good."

"Oh, you always look good to me. In fact, you look great. But, I have to go food shopping first."

"Before you go, I need to ask you something," Katherine said carefully. "Why did you decide on 'David' for the baby's name?"

"I don't know. I think I simply like the name," he answered.

"I like it, too. But, may we consider changing it?"

"To what?"

"I don't know."

"How about 'Lloyd'?" he asked as convincingly as possible.

"Are you serious?" Katherine asked with a smile. She is completely caught by surprise.

"Of course I am. 'Lloyd' is a fine name," he offered with a broad grin. Jacob grabs his cane. He grips the handle very tightly; he imagines breaking it over her head. "We'll make those changes soon. But, for now, let me go shopping."

"Please hurry back."

He gives her a kiss on the lips. To her, the act is passionate. However, he imagined liberating her lips from her face in one bite and then spitting the bloody remnants into her eyes. He then leaves through the back door and walks into the garage. There, he obtains the splitting ax; he sharpened it again the night before. He takes it with him. He also takes a filled duffle bag that was also waiting for him in the garage.

After driving for about an hour, he reaches his destination. He parks his car far enough to prevent detection. It is a rather luxurious home in an upscale town nestled around a huge lake. In the driveway, he sees an expensive sports car parked near the sizable front door. He steps out of his car using the ax as a makeshift cane while abandoning his cane in the car. He carries the duffle bag with him. He walks the distance slowly and carefully, never leaving sight of the front door. He steps up to it; the edifice is noticeably ornate and features a letter "V" conspicuously mounted over the large, brass knocker. As he rings the doorbell, he carefully conceals the heavy implement under his armpit. The door opens.

"Colton, old friend! How are you?" Jacob said with a cheesy grin.

"Why, Jacob. What are you doing here?" Colton said in a weak voice. "Is everything all right?"

"Fine, fine. Say, may I come in for a moment?"

"Well, I was just getting ready to leave," Colton said while looking away for a moment.

"Don't worry, I won't linger." Jacob steps in nearly pushing Colton back. He then closes the door behind him before Colton can see the ax. Jacob then picks up the ax and presses the head of it against Colton's chest and pushes him back further and further.

"I heard about your wife, and I just wanted to stop by." Jacob takes a deep breath. "To offer my condolences."

"Now see here! What is this all about?"

"I saw your wife, by the way. She has long hair, and a pretty face. Not much of a body, though."

Jacob pushes Colton against the wall with the ax.

"Don't make me call the police!"

"Sit," Jacob quietly commands. "Just sit."

Colton reluctantly complies.

"Now, I don't know what this is all about," Colton said; "so..."

"Shh!" Jacob interrupted. "I believe—now this is just a theory mind you—that you've been fucking my Katherine," he said in an almost singsong manner.

"Wha—? What are you talking about? I—I..."

"In fact, the baby is yours! Congrats, daddy!"

"But I didn't have sex with your wife! I swear it!" Colton pleaded.

"You deliberately enticed her, you fucked her, and then, bang, baby! Do I really need to give you a biology lesson? Come on!"

"I didn't!"

"Oh, and your wife's 'accident' was rather convenient," Jacob said while indicating quotes with his fingers. "Tell me, what did you do? Put a small hole in her brake fluid tank, perhaps? Drip, drip, drip. Eventually, she steps on the brake and..."

"You're mad! You're fucking mad!" Colton screamed while gripping the chair's armrests.

Jacob quickly lifts the ax and wields it. Colton's head flies clean off. Blood propels upward nearly drenching the entire room. The head rolls toward Jacob. In its last bit of animation, the face holds a grimace while the lips slightly tremble and then become still.

"Wow! Elvis has left the building!" Jacob said while raising the bloodied ax. He is considerably drenched. "You know, Colton, I didn't know you can do impressions. And, that was a pretty good one."

Jacob retrieves the duffle bag from outside. Before he goes back in, he takes a quick look around. No one is in sight; he closes the door. He brings the bag into a bathroom and unzips it. It contains a clean set of dinner clothes, his meth case, and a large plastic bag.

"Say, Colton ol' buddy?" he called out from the bathroom. "You don't mind if I take a shower, do you?" He looks around. "I must say, this is one hell-of-a bathroom. Are these gold fixtures, you fuck? My father-in-law must be paying you real well."

After the shower, he injects himself, packs his things and gets dressed.

"Hey, Colton, I'm going to head out now. Take care, pal. No need to get up. I'll just leave through the back."

Jacob puts the duffle bag and the cleaned ax in the trunk and heads off to the market. He called there in advance to order a special pork loin roast for tonight's special dinner.

* * *

"Babe, I'm home!" Jacob said while carrying in bags of groceries.

"Okay, honey!" Katherine said. "What took you so long?"

"Oh, the market was so crowded, and the lines were so long."

"I have just enough time to go to the hairdresser."

"Just go," he said with a smile. "I'll take care of things." He sees the baby sitting in the highchair. "Hey, David—I mean, Lloyd."

Katherine kisses Jacob and hurries off.

Jacob removes the pork loin roast from the butcher paper and lays it on the counter. He then removes a huge butcher knife from the knife holder.

* * *

Katherine comes home rather late. But, she returns before her parents arrive.

"Your hair looks great!" Jacob said.

"Oh, thanks! And, the roast smells amazing."

"Baby Lloyd is upstairs sleeping for the night. I have the monitor here." Jacob points to it on the kitchen counter.

After a few minutes, the doorbell rings. Katherine greets her parents at the door.

"Mom, dad! Come in!"

"Hello, dear!" Constance said. They embrace. "Where's my baby grandson?"

"He's upstairs sleeping. Maybe I'll bring him down if he wakes up. Hi, dad!" Katherine embraces him.

* * *

At the dining table before dinner, no one is saying much. They sip wine and make small talk. Constance mentions how pretty the flowers look in the vase, and then attempts to lift spirits by recognizing the special occasion.

"Congratulates on your wedding anniversary!" She raises her glass.

Lloyd rolls his eyes.

"Thanks, mom." Katherine looks at Jacob. "Let's serve dinner now."

"I'll take care of that," Jacob insisted.

While Jacob is in the kitchen, Lloyd shifts in his seat. Katherine notices.

"Dad, what's wrong?" Katherine asked.

"Oh, don't mind him," Constance said. "He's just hungry."

"I'm starving," Lloyd grumbled. "Your mother had me running around all day."

Jacob returns with plates of food.

"Well, it's about time," Lloyd said.

"Now, ladies first!" Jacob said to him playfully.

"Oh, it looks delicious," Constance said.

Jacob goes back into the kitchen and immediately returns with a plate for Lloyd.

"Right here," Lloyd said while raising his hand.

"On the way." Jacob placed a plate of food in front of him.

"I gave you an extra helping of pork, Lloyd."

"Oh, Kate," Lloyd said with a smile; "Colton says hello."

"Oh, that's nice," Katherine said with some discomfort.

"He is such a great guy." Lloyd picks up a forkful of meat. "I recently gave him a raise. I truly admire that man. You should call him."

"Dad, please?" Katherine scolded.

"I'm just saying," he retorted. "A truly admirable man."

"No, it's okay," Jacob insisted to Katherine. "Your dad's right: He's a good guy. He's... *admirable*, yeah."

"Oh, dad," Katherine said with enthusiasm; "Jacob has some good news for you."

"No, babe, you tell him," Jacob said.

"Well, um," Katherine takes a breath; "Jacob and I decided to change the name of our baby."

"Really," Constance said with a smile.

"Our son is now named Lloyd," Katherine said while nearly tearing up.

"Oh, that's great!" Constance said to Lloyd. "Isn't that great?"

"Yeah, great," Lloyd said with little interest. "Next, we have to work on the last name."

"Ha-ha!" Jacob laughed. "Lloyd, that's funny, really. And, I know you appreciate that we named our baby after you."

"Lots to celebrate," Constance added.

There is a moment when no words are exchanged. We hear only the sound of chewing.

"Mm, Katie, dear, you outdid yourself with this roast," Constance said while still chewing.

"Yeah, Kate, his roast is so succulent," Lloyd said with a mouth full of meat.

"Jacob cooked, dad," Katherine said.

"It's so aromatic," Constance said.

"That's the rosemary," Jacob boasted.

"Well, Jacob, maybe you should start wearing a skirt, too," Lloyd quipped.

"Hey, we forgot to say grace," Jacob said. "Let me: God, thank you for what we are receiving, and thank you for baby Lloyd. Amen."

Katherine smiles at Jacob. The others continue eating. Jacob grins and folds his hands in front of his mouth.

"Honey, why aren't you eating?" Katherine asked.

"I'm not really hungry, darling," he answered. "In fact, I'm real tired and I think I'll go to bed."

"Okay, dear. I'll be up soon."

"Good-night, all. Love you!" Jacob said with a smile as he stood. Katherine blows a kiss. Constance smiles back. Lloyd continues eating and never looks up.

Before he turns to go upstairs, Jacob takes a good look at everyone. His smile never left his face.

* * *

Katherine waves to the Whittendams from below the veranda. After she sees them drive off, she goes inside and considers cleaning up in the morning. She does manage to bring some plates into the kitchen. While there, she sees a large, covered roasting pan sitting on the stove. She thinks of how fortunate she is to have married such a good cook. More importantly, she notices that Jacob is much less stressed, and she is glad that he has been showing her more affection. He has been trying real hard. She truly believes that their marriage is finally headed in the right direction, and that they have been blessed with a healthy son. She knows now that baby Lloyd is a product of their love and proof of God's gift to them.

She then looks down on the counter and on the floor and notices some blood droplets. She hoped that Jacob did not somehow cut himself. She wipes up the blood.

She then goes upstairs to the baby's room to check on him. She is glad that he has been sleeping so soundly. When she looks in the crib and rolls back the covers, underneath she finds the raw pork loin roast.

Katherine screams.

Chapter Twelve

"What did you do?" Katherine exclaimed.

"I made dinner for you and your parents," Jacob snickered.

"What did you do to our baby? You killed our baby?"

"It's not my baby. It was never my baby!"

"What are you talking about?"

"It's Colton's, isn't it?" Jacob approaches her.

"What are you saying? It's your baby! Are you crazy? Colton means nothing to me. I've always been faithful to you!"

Katherine begins to go mad. She runs downstairs as Jacob steadily follows her. She runs into the kitchen and looks at the roasting pan. She stares at it for a moment and considers picking up the lid, and then she vomits. She regains some composure, and then retrieves a large kitchen knife. As she turns, she sees Jacob standing near her. She points the knife at him.

"You stay away from me!" she screamed.

"C'mon, Katherine," Jacob said while slowly walking toward her. "Let's start over. This time, we'll have a child of our own—like it was meant to be. We can even name him Lloyd if you want."

"Stay away!"

"And, we won't have to worry about Colton getting in the way any longer; I took care of that."

"I'll kill you! Y-you stay away from me!"

"Put down the knife, Katherine."

"NO!"

"Put down the knife."

Katherine charges Jacob pointing the knife at him, but he overpowers her. He turns the knife on her and presses the blade against her neck.

"Bad wifey," Jacob whispered into her ear.

He then slits her throat. As the blood pours out of her, she loses consciousness. He releases her and she falls to the floor. He carefully places the knife on the counter and then takes a deep breath. He sees a glass with some wine still in it. He finishes it. He then drags Katherine's lifeless body through the back door to the rear yard with the intention of burying her in the garden.

* * *

Katherine's body lies in the garden under a bright moon. After Jacob dug a hole to bury her body, he sits on the mound of dirt to catch his breath. He considers withdrawing all of his and Katherine's monies in the morning and escaping overseas, maybe to Asia. He thinks of all the mistakes that he has made and all of the trust that he lost in the people that he loved. He realized that he had to put himself first.

He stands and walks to Katherine's body. He bends over to pick her up. Just as he does, the weeds surrounding her come to life and take hold of her body. He attempts to lift her, but he cannot.

"What the fuck?" he exclaimed.

More weeds crop up from the ground under Jacob and take hold of his feet. He gasps. Just then, an arm emerges from the ground and grabs his injured leg. He screams and forcefully pulls his leg away. He pulls so hard that he falls to the ground. He is freed. He attempts to rise, but the wound on his leg has opened and it begins to bleed. He sees the arm protruding from the ground toward him; the hand is opening and closing.

"Fuck you!" he screamed at it.

He manages to crawl out of the garden. When he looks back, he sees Adeline Cole emerge from the ground in her burial dress. She reveals to him her grotesque form. Jacob screams in fear.

Ignoring the pain, he stands and retreats back into the house. He is so panic-stricken that he slams into a wall. When he sees the flowers that Katherine picked from the garden in a vase on the dining table, they immediately wither and die before his eyes. He then immediately turns and is confronted by Thomas Cole.

There doesn't seem to be any life in Thomas's eyes. He is quite deformed; his head appears limp and it is resting on his shoulders because his neck is broken. As dead as Thomas looks, he is quite alert and very strong. He takes hold of Jacob and drags him to the parlor. Above them, tethered to the central beam, is a long rope with a noose carefully tied at the bottom.

"This is how it must be," Thomas said slowly.

"What? Let me go!" Jacob insisted.

Thomas climbs on to a small table and lifts Jacob. He forces Jacob's neck through the noose. He wraps his arms around Jacob.

"NO!" Jacob screamed.

Thomas leaps off the table holding Jacob. The rope catches. After Jacob struggles for a moment, his neck snaps and he expires. As soon as this happens, the garage door outside quickly opens and the 1957 Chevrolet's engine starts. Thomas takes down Jacob's body and leaves the noose dangling. He drags Jacob's lifeless body out the back door and to the car. He tosses the body into the trunk. He then retrieves Katherine's body and also tosses it into the trunk. He then sits in the driver's seat.

Adeline walks out of the garden carrying her disfigured baby and sits in the passenger seat. Thomas gives Adeline a careful kiss on her bare teeth and smiles down at the baby in her lap. Before Thomas shifts gears, Lorenzo emerges from the garden, still with his gaping chest wound from Jacob, and while holding the head of Colton's wife. He gets into the back seat of the Chevrolet without muttering a word. He carefully adjusts the head on his lap while it looks up at him and smiles. Lorenzo smiles back. They all drive off and, as the car reaches the end of the driveway, it quietly disappears. Gone.

Epilogue

"Come this way, folks! Step inside!" Mr. Lewis directed while puffing on a cigarette. "Oh, I'm sorry ma'am; I see that you're pregnant, so let me toss this."

Mr. Lewis flicks the cigarette on to the ground. It lands near a pile of the dry leaves.

"Welcome to Seven Oaks!" Mr. Lewis offers a broad grin. "It features Queen Anne Revival style architecture, and it was built in 1914—back when they knew how to build houses, right? It's three stories of some the nicest rooms that you may ever see. So, is this your first?" he asked while gesturing to the wife's protuberance.

"It's our first," the wife said.

"We're four months away," the husband said with enthusiasm while rubbing his wife's abdomen.

"Splendid! It's a great house to raise a family, I assure you."

The tour of the house ends in the kitchen.

"Let's go check out the yard," Mr. Lewis said while never abandoning his smile.

As they step outside through the back door, Mr. Lewis gestures.

"You have a garden to plant whatever your heart desires," Mr. Lewis said. "And, that's the garage. It's the newest structure on the property. I think you'll find it spacious enough."

They step up to the garage door windows, but they cannot see inside.

"May I open it?" the husband asked.

"Certainly." Mr. Lewis assists him. They raise the door high. Before them, in the center of the space they see a large, canvassed-covered object. When the cover is removed, there sits the 1957 Chevrolet.

"I guess they never drove it," Mr. Lewis almost said to himself.

"What do you mean?" the husband asked.

"I mean, I guess it's a car the previous owners left." Mr. Lewis recovered. "Gee, it sure is a beaut, huh!"

"Does this car come with the house?" the wife asked.

"It sure does," Mr. Lewis answered with a slight giggle. "And, look, the keys are in the ignition."

"May I start her up?" the husband asked.

"Ah, sure," Mr. Lewis said with some hesitancy in his voice.

When the key is turned, the engine starts right up.

"Woo-hoo!" the husband said with his arms raised. "It's such a nice car; I wonder why they left it."

"It beats the hell out of me," Mr. Lewis said.

"How long has this house been on the market?" the wife asked.

"Um, it's been vacant for about two years—it has great potential," Mr. Lewis said.

"What happened with the previous owners?" the husband asked.

"They moved after living here for a year, I think. Their marriage wasn't going right and—well, let's just say it's a real horror story."

"Well, we sure do love the place," the wife said.

"Yeah, we sure do," the husband said while looking into his wife's eyes.

The couple seems very enamored with the property, and the purchase appears imminent.

The very last image, as we move away from the handshakes, is that of the forward-facing gable. It features the frieze of a grinning cherub.